A
Harlequin
Romance

OTHER
Harlequin Romances
by KATRINA BRITT

Many of these titles are available at your local bookseller
or through the Harlequin Reader Service.

For a free catalogue listing all available Harlequin Romances,
send your name and address to:

HARLEQUIN READER SERVICE,
M.P.O. Box 707, Niagara Falls, N.Y. **14302**
Canadian address: Stratford, Ontario, Canada N5A 6W4

or use order coupon at back of book.

TAKE BACK
YOUR LOVE

by

KATRINA BRITT

HARLEQUIN BOOKS

TORONTO
WINNIPEG

Harlequin edition published September 1975

SBN 373-01906-8

Original hard cover edition published in 1975
by Mills & Boon Limited.

All the characters in this book have no existence outside the
imagination of the Author, and have no relation whatsoever to
anyone bearing the same name or names. They are not even
distantly inspired by any individual known or unknown to the
Author, and all the incidents are pure invention.

Printed in Canada

1906

CHAPTER ONE

THE taxi swayed perilously, ploughing its way through the traffic and narrowly missing bicycles, cars and buses at such an erratic speed that poor Annabel began to wonder whether she would ever reach her destination all in one piece. The magic of her surroundings, the strange yellow faces, the mothers with their babies strapped on to their backs, the pretty diminutive dolly girls enchanting in kimonos and Western dress and the old men clip-clopping along in their wooden getas, were as unreal as the nightmare journey.

Aunt Bea's address had been written down in Japanese for Annabel to give to the taxi driver whom she had hired on her arrival in Tokyo.

'It's almost impossible to find an address in Tokyo,' Aunt Bea had written, 'so I am enclosing my address to give to the taxi driver in case I am too late returning from my holiday abroad to meet you when you arrive.'

Dear Aunt Bea! Annabel thought fondly of her aunt who at the age of forty-five was branching out as a successful writer of crime fiction. She had settled down in Japan two years after going there on a visit to gather material for a new book.

Japan had been a country she had known little about, but from the moment she had arrived, Aunt Bea had felt at home. She had fallen in love with a country which had appealed enormously to her artistic nature and had found it the ideal place in which to write.

Annabel had missed her terribly at first, for she had

5

grown up with Aunt Bea and Grandmother Stacey. Her own parents, concert singers, toured the continent and were often away from home. Consequently Annabel, an only child, had been left in the care of her father's mother and sister until she had qualified as an accountant and taken a flat in London. It had been round about this time that Grandmother Stacey had died leaving Aunt Bea, who had refused countless offers of marriage in order to look after her mother, alone.

Her first novel had been written through the years and put away in a drawer. She had come across it when clearing out the house which was put up for sale and had sent it to a publisher. It had been accepted and now, two years later, she was becoming a celebrity in the crime fiction world.

'You must come to stay with me, Annabel,' she had written. 'You'll love it here. Besides, I haven't seen you for two years, not since you went to Paris to spend a holiday with your mother and father. Now it's my turn. So do come.'

Was it only two years since that memorable holiday in Paris? Annabel's mouth thinned at the thought. John and Anne Stacey had been engaged for the season at one of the famous night clubs in Paris and Annabel had gone to spend a holiday with them. Much as she loved her parents, she had bitterly rued the decision to go to see them, for it was in Paris that she had met Pierre Devigne.

Pierre was a dashing up-to-the-minute journalist who had stolen her heart at their first meeting, and Annabel had never felt the same since. On that memorable evening she had been seated at a table at the night club where her parents joined her after going through their act when Pierre Devigne had strode in.

An arresting figure, tall, tanned and around thirty-five with a thick mop of black hair, he had appeared blissfully unaware of the feminine heads turning his way as he entered the room.

There was an alert intelligence in his gaze, a sureness in him that made Annabel thrillingly aware of him. His rather saturnine features were not classically symmetrical. His best friend would not have called him handsome, for his face was too rough-hewn. Yet there had been something dramatically compelling about him, a masculine ugliness which added rather than detracted from his appearance, giving him a strength of character.

When he had taken a table opposite to her on the other side of the cleared floor space, she had felt his presence like a kind of built-in radar. But it had been clear that she was not his type, for he had not spared her one glance, although he had only to lift his head and gaze across the room.

Annabel, recalling her own reflection in the wall mirror of the room, had not been surprised that he had not noticed her. Apart from her neat, glossy dark hair and long-lashed deep blue eyes, her features were not outstanding. Her face was too pale, a pure milky white, her small nose negligible and her mouth ordinary.

But if Pierre Devigne had not noticed her the three young Frenchmen who had taken the table next to her had. They had taken their places with an unsteady gait as though they had already partaken of too much wine, and while they waited for their order they tried to catch Annabel's attention.

Forewarned by their inebriated appearance and the way one of them had deliberately stumbled very near to her on arrival, she had looked the other way very

7

carefully. Then one of the bolder ones had come across unsteadily to her table.

Pierre had looked across at that moment, mildly interested to watch Annabel shake her head at the young man's request for her to join them. When he had seen the young man bend down to whisper something in her ear jeeringly, he had been contemptuously amused. He had not heard what had been said, but he blamed Annabel entirely for creating the situation by dining alone. A pale doll-like creature, had been his first impression, with the fragility of an early Victorian miss who would probably swoon at the mere suggestion of passion.

Then suddenly the expression of fright on her face had awakened all his latent chivalry. His dark eyes took on a fiery gleam which actually glowed like live coals when he was really roused. Quietly with a loose-limbed grace of an outdoor man he had moved fast with no appearance of haste to her table.

'*Allez!*' he had commanded the young man. 'This lady is already booked.'

He had spoken in French and the next few seconds had hung on an ugly thread when the bold young man had looked up at him insolently. But what he had seen of Pierre's fitness and his fine physique had finally convinced him that it was politic to withdraw.

Dropping into the chair opposite to Annabel at the table, Pierre had addressed her in almost unaccented English.

'Please do not think I am being fresh like our young friend. You do not have to have my company in exchange if you do not wish to. I shall not be offended if you ask me to go away—although it would be wiser in the circumstances for you to dine with me.'

Annabel had experienced a feeling of him being

8

sociable against his will. He was evidently a man's man—or he could be married. For some reason she could not explain a warm wave of colour flooded her clear skin and she had lowered her eyes.

'I would like you to stay, please,' she had told him quietly, and had gone on to explain what she was doing sitting alone.

Later, he had met her parents, had been obviously charmed by them and had been absolutely charming himself. Annabel had learned that he was a bachelor and a journalist taking a respite between assignments.

He had been her companion for the rest of her holiday and she had seen Paris through his eyes. He had been born there and he loved it. No one could have had a more exciting or amusing companion. Annabel had never met anyone like Pierre. His assignments had taken him all over the world to all the war-ravaged countries of Europe and his slant on life was consequently hard and cynical. Yet he had the most disarming smile and a nonchalant charm which wrought havoc with her unwary heart.

Her blue eyes had widened with wonder and tenderness until they began to shine with love. She had lived in an unreal world of ecstasy from which she had been rudely and somewhat forcibly awakened. It had been her own fault entirely, for Pierre had never deliberately set out to win her love. Hard and cynical he might be, but there had not been the slightest hint of meanness in his whole make-up. Her parents had liked him very much and had left her in his care knowing he was a man of integrity.

Annabel shivered on remembered pain and gave her attention to the passing scenery, curling her hands around the edge of her seat as they bounced over potholes in the road. They had left the city behind and

9

the roads were lined with cherry and cryptomeria trees which reminded her of Paris. She recalled the happy excursions with Pierre into the suburbs, boarding a *bateau mouche* among a merry crowd of students and *grisettes* en route for Meudon or St Cloud.

There had always been someone on board with an accordion or a guitar for the inevitable jolly get-together, and they had all sung with gusto and the joy of being young. On her last evening Pierre had taken her on the river in a small boat. There had been a firework display and they had watched multi-coloured rockets shooting up into the dark blue velvet sky to fall in showers of burning rain on to the water.

That night had been Paris in one of her most romantic moods, with a full moon smiling down at its own reflection on the river. Annabel had drifted along in a wonderland of soft music and laughter mingling with the soft splash of the oars on the water.

Pierre had sat opposite her, rowing lazily and watching the enchantment of her small face. Pale as the moon smiling down on them, she had felt his magnetism, finding love as wonderful as she had dreamed it would be and feeling heaven very near. The soft evening breeze had caressed the tendrils of hair curling around her forehead and her blue eyes had been wide and luminous in the sudden flare of the rockets as she watched their progress.

He had been watching her intently, meeting her questioning gaze with tender amusement. Earlier that evening, they had dined and danced together, with Annabel trying to face the fact that she might never see him again after that night. The mere thought of it had been so agonising that she had looked at him as he rowed with a poignant appeal which his eagle eyes had not missed.

10

He had shaken his head, his smile protective and sad.

'It would not work, *ma petite chère*. Not you and I.'

Annabel had started nervously. Utterly disconcerted, she had put a small hand to her face, felt it burn and had said an outrageous thing.

'I love you, Pierre.'

The words had been spoken quite simply as though it had been the most natural admission in the world and that it had been necessary to tell him.

And Pierre had answered with his dark brows tilted into a pained frown.

'*Mais pourquoi pas, chérie?* You are in love with love. Do you not know that Paris is a Circe who weaves an aura of romance around unsuspecting visitors and deludes them into seeing everything through rose-coloured spectacles?'

Annabel had kept her eyes on his dark face, wondering what he had thought of her outspokenness, her lack of pride in throwing herself at him. But she had not cared what he had thought. She had to know the truth of how he felt about her.

'Then you don't love me?'

Her voice had been a small husky whisper hanging in the silence as Pierre had rowed the boat towards the bank of the river. Almost imperceptibly, he drew in the oars and reached for her hands. The next moment she had been sitting beside him with his arm around her as she leaned back against his chest.

Then he had spoken softly to her as to a child. 'I love you enough to put your happiness first. You would never be happy with me and the life I lead. I'm a rolling stone, stopping between assignments only long enough to refresh myself for the next. Sometimes

11

I find myself in situations where I have little hope of getting out alive. Do not tremble so much, *mignonne*. You are far too sensible to break your precious heart over a man like me. I am not worth it.'

'Oh, darling Pierre!'

A brief silence followed the piteous entreaty until Annabel had felt that the beating of her heart would choke her. Then had come the touch of his lips upon her hair and its wild throbbing grew calmer.

'No, *ma petite*! I know what I am talking about, believe me. I am a man of the world. Try to treat this as a casual holiday affair, will you? I have had affairs, but the only lasting one is my work. So you will put your love for me into the past tense. Will you not? Then I shall not feel so hellish about it.'

Annabel had not answered. Her blue eyes had been swimming with tears which she had been trying valiantly to blink away.

'You will. Promise me.'

She had twisted then in his hold to look up at him, her eyes wide and steadfast.

'I'll try,' she had said.

He had regarded her intently with the old derisive lines still on his face. '*Eh bien*, then no harm has been done.' He had uttered the words with the familiar dancing raillery in his eyes and had bent his head. His kiss, tender though it had been, had not been the kiss of a lover. It had been as baffling as his smile.

As she recalled it, Annabel's soft mouth tightened. She held tightly to the edge of her seat as the taxi swerved around a corner on to a road lined with stately elms. High hedges concealed the houses behind them. They were set on the hillside overlooking the bay and the little fishing village clustered below. There was an alpine touch about it until, driving in between carved wooden gates, the illusion was swept away as they drove through a Japanese garden.

Everything dear to the heart of the Japanese was there, water trickling over stones laid with loving artistry, bamboo bridges, stone lanterns, weeping willow and the fan-shaped foliage of palms and magnolia.

The house spread itself over soft green lawns in sleepy silence broken only by the twittering of birds. A reddish purple bougainvillaea had climbed over the porch entrance—and suddenly there was Aunt Bea. Tall and slender, she wore a shantung silk trouser suit. There were pearl studs in her ears and a matching pearl necklace around her throat. The slim brown hand she held out was graced by a beautiful cameo ring.

'Annabel darling!' she exclaimed. 'So sorry I couldn't meet you. I've only just arrived myself. How are you? Did you have a good journey?'

They kissed warmly, and Annabel decided that her aunt looked far younger than her age with her tanned face framed by brown hair in pageboy style. It suited her piquant face and her warm brown eyes were studying the features of her niece, noting the violet shadows beneath the dark blue eyes.

Annabel laughed. 'I had a marvellous journey,' she declared. 'What about you?'

'So-so.'

Aunt Bea paid the taxi driver, and as he left a yellow-skinned young man with jet black hair and shoebutton eyes came from the house. He was a handsome young man with dancing eyes and very correct in a white jacket over black trousers. His smile was white as he bowed before relieving Annabel of her cream travelling coat which she carried on her arm.

Aunt Bea introduced him as he was about to pick up

Annabel's suitcases.

'This is Deno, my helper and friend. I don't know what I should do without him.' She put an arm around Annabel's slim shoulders. 'Deno, here is my niece at last.'

His low bow revealed the back of his neatly trimmed black hair. Then he was off smiling with her suitcases.

In the vestibule between the two front doors, they slipped off their shoes to put on the house slippers provided.

'I've become used to changing my shoes when I enter the house,' her aunt said. 'It's a good habit to cultivate because it keeps the interior of the house so clean and sparkling.'

The hall was light and sunny. The zebra rugs on the polished wooden floor went perfectly with the collection of antique weapons displayed on the walls. An expanse of polished floor was a superb foil in the lounge for the off-white rugs where sliding glass doors along one wall opened out on to a patio overlooking the garden. A curved white leather-buttoned suite arrayed with gay cushions blended delightfully with the few exquisite pieces of daintily carved furniture in dark wood against neutral walls.

Annabel stood entranced at the fine old paintings on the walls and the beautiful flower arrangements.

'What a light happy house, Aunt Bea,' she declared. 'I love the way this room overlooks the garden.'

'All the rooms have a view. I prefer a house to a bungalow because I like sleeping upstairs.' With her hand thrust through Annabel's arm she piloted her upstairs into a pretty bedroom where Deno had already put her suitcases. Annabel saw a bedroom suite in white wood where neutral walls and pretty flowered window curtains complemented the matching bed-spread and white shaggy wool rugs on the polished floor to give a restful look.

Aunt Bea said fondly, 'I'm sure you're hot and sticky after your journey. Would you like a bath now or after lunch?'

'A bath, please.'

'Then I'll see you later in the lounge.'

When her aunt had departed Annabel walked to the window opening out on to a veranda. Walking on to it, she stared out at the distant view of the bay beyond the garden. Towards the horizon unknown peninsulas and pretty villages rose from the water. Offshore below children were swimming in the blue water, their delighted cries tossed away mutedly through blue-green pines lining the slopes. The air smelt of wood smoke and human fertilizer, an aroma that was to become all too familiar to her during her stay.

Annabel sighed. Well, here she was thousands of miles away from Pierre, wherever he might be. Surely the sense of distance, of being in an entirely different world away from him, would exorcise his memory? Yet time had not, so how could distance? Annabel swallowed on remembered pain, clenched her hands and stiffened her slim shoulders. She would enjoy her holiday, Pierre or no Pierre. She was determined upon that.

In the blue and white tiled bathroom with its cunningly placed mirrors giving an air of spaciousness, Annabel lingered in a fragrant bath. Later, feeling wonderfully refreshed, she slipped on a cool linen dress and went downstairs to the lounge. They dined on the patio on white bamboo furniture where green cushions matched the glass-topped table. Lunch was served cold and was delicious.

'Japanese food,' commented Bea, 'is more decorative than enjoyable—at least, I find it so. So I settle for the food I'm used to. Some of my English and American friends here insist that Japanese food is delightful. Yet whenever I visit them it's never served.' She helped herself to egg salad. 'What do you think of the tea?'

Annabel savoured the aromatic green tea served in a small handleless cup. 'Different from our own, of course, but very refreshing.'

Bea nodded. 'I've developed a liking for it—which is more than I can say for the soups. I can't stand those unidentifiable little objects floating on the top with no specific flavour to speak of. However, some of the dishes are enjoyable and Tokyo has an extensive range of eating places, most of them excellent, as you'll discover.'

Over a cigarette at the end of their meal, Bea said, 'What about a short stroll to digest our meal? Or are you too tired after your journey?'

Annabel smiled. 'What about you? You had a long journey too.'

'I'm not tired. Flapping my wings after being fastened in with Mother all those years stimulates me. Besides, I want to use up the last of the film in my camera so that I can take it to be developed.'

They strolled along the drive, out through the double gates and along a road sloping downwards towards the little bay. The air was hot as they picked their way down to the sea wall overlooking the quiet curve of sea and sand. Boats were pulled up on the shingle of sheltered coves and the arthritic limbs of dark trees preened over rocks to see their reflections in the blue water. Annabel sat on the sea wall for her aunt to take a snap of her. The camera clicked on the

16

adorable profile of her niece.

'Now I want one with a smile, please.'

When Annabel had obliged, Bea spoke to her camera as she returned it to her shoulder case. 'That smile you gave was loaded with pathos. You've changed, Annabel. You've lost that sparkle, that zest for life radiating from you like the sun. What's happened to it?'

Annabel slipped down from the sea wall and tried to sound casual as they continued their way down to the sea.

'One does change a little in two years, Aunt Bea,' she said reasonably.

'Would you say I've changed?' dryly.

Annabel studied the still youthful profile of her aunt. 'Dear Aunt Bea! You'll never change. If anything you look younger.' She thrust an arm into that of the older woman.

'Thanks. Now what's changed you? I was given to understand by your letters that you loved your job, your flat and everything.'

'I do.'

'Then since you're not telling me to mind my own business, I'll hazard a guess. You want to live in Paris with your parents but can't make up your mind to leave your job and your friends?'

Annabel, off guard, replied more vehemently than she would have wished. 'Oh no! Paris is the last place I would choose.' She recovered herself quickly, feeling her aunt's enquiring eyes on her flushed profile. 'I have no wish to live anywhere other than London.'

Bea frowned, not entirely convinced. 'What have you against Paris? I know your parents would love to have you with them, and I thought you enjoyed your holiday there.'

17

'I did. But I love my flat and my job and I'm not giving them up,' Annabel said firmly.

'Until you marry.'

'I suppose so,' she answered almost without expression.

'You don't sound very enthusiastic about marriage,' Bea teased her.

'You've got along all right without it,' defensively.

Bea swivelled a startled glance towards her. 'Good heavens, child, don't model yourself on me. My single state is none of my own choosing—not that I would consider marriage now. I've been a prisoner too long not to appreciate my freedom. I also have a very rewarding job in writing.'

In the silence which followed the subject was dropped and during the rest of their walk Bea talked about her visit to America. As they retraced their steps up the mountain paths she pointed out a yacht club and several split-level villas gracing the hillside.

'The Firbanks, American friends of mine, live there,' Bea vouchsafed, indicating a high-powered American car in the drive of one of the more opulent villas. 'You'll like them. They're dining with us this evening.'

She smiled down affectionately at Annabel, wishing she knew what was making her look so sad. Bea was a poor correspondent. After slogging away at her typewriter letter-writing was a chore she could well do without. Now she was wishing that she had written more often to John and Anne, Annabel's parents, who would probably have enlightened her about what was troubling their daughter. Despite being a writer of crime fiction, Bea was an incurable romantic.

Her niece was the kind of young woman to invite thoughts of romance, being dainty and demure, swift to blush and tremulous of smile. She was the kind men would want to cherish and protect. Bea was surprised that she had no ring on her finger, for she must have had her share of admirers during her two years spent at the office.

How old was Annabel now? Twenty-one? An ideal age to marry and settle down with the right man. Aunt Bea decided in that moment that she would have to do something about it.

That evening when Annabel went down to dinner the guests had already arrived. They were a typical American couple, frank and friendly. Dick Firbank had a long, lean, narrow parchment-like face, a man in his forties with receding fair hair and good teeth. His handclasp was hearty and firm as he greeted Annabel with appraisal.

Ella, his wife, was remarkably like him, rather tall and well made, almost angular, with warm sherry-coloured eyes in a tanned face. Annabel found them both likeable and they chatted over a sherry, Bea consulting her wristwatch from time to time.

At last she set down her empty glass and addressed Ella: 'You did say Marilyn was coming with a friend?'

Ella looked embarrassed. 'My goodness, yes. The minx is late again. I'm sorry, Bea. She did promise to be on time, but you know what she is.' Her smile at Bea was pathetic. 'We've spoiled our daughter terribly and this is the result. Do forgive her. I'm not as upset as I know I ought to be. You see, she's found a new escort, a really nice guy, and we're hoping for miracles —aren't we, Dad?'

Ella looked hopefully towards her husband, who nodded his head. But Bea was not impressed.

'I'm sorry, we simply can't put dinner off any

longer. Deno must be worried stiff in case everything is spoiled by the delay. I . . .'

In that moment the sound of a car stopping outside the house cut in on what Bea was about to say. There was an expectant silence and all eyes turned towards the door, which was opened by Deno.

'Miss Marilyn Firbank and Mr Pierre Devigne,' he said on a deep bow.

A young woman appeared in the doorway. She was slim and leggy with long-lashed grey-green eyes and blonde hair. Her mouth was curved into a smile and she was very attractive in an arresting, defiant kind of way.

She came forward gracefully speaking on an apologetic note.

'I'm so sorry, Aunt Bea, for being late,' she said in the rather affected tones of a spoilt child. 'It was all my fault. I insisted upon Pierre taking me to Picture Island and we forget the time. Pierre, come and be introduced.'

Annabel's heart leapt and beat suffocatingly as Pierre Devigne strolled nonchalantly into the room. She had the sensation of diving into icy water and surfacing in an attempt to fill her lungs with air. For what seemed an age, she stared at him, separated by a whole world of two years. He was the same Pierre of the tanned features and mobile mouth. Only he seemed to be leaner—too lean—as though he had been under pressure of some kind.

He greeted the Firbanks with a lazy charm, holding out a lean brown hand to Bea before turning to Annabel. Apart from regarding her humorously he showed no emotion whatever at their unexpected meeting. His careless approach gave her the composure she needed to put the correct amount of pleasure and surprise into

20

her voice.

'Pierre! How nice to see you again. This is an unexpected pleasure.'

She put out her hand, wishing it was not trembling so much, and felt his hard fingers close around it coolly.

His dark eyes appraised her. 'Annabel! Still as sweet as ever. How are you?'

'Quite well, thanks. I've grown up in the last two years,' she answered meaningly before gently disengaging her hand from his clasp and turning to Bea. 'Pierre and I met two years ago when I went to visit Mummy and Daddy in Paris. He was kind enough to show me around. He also rescued me from a very sticky situation.'

Annabel felt Marilyn's grey-green eyes fixed upon her in a smile of amusement. It was a smile without malice and Annabel felt strangely drawn to the girl, who was about the same age as herself. There was something about her on closer inspection, a sweet childlike candour of one who had been cushioned against the sharp corners of life and found it vastly amusing.

'There you see, Mother,' she commented, turning to Ella. 'You were quite right about Pierre being a knight errant.'

Ella was not amused. Her sallow face suffused with colour. 'You talk too much, you tiresome child. Aunt Bea is waiting for us to go in to dinner.'

Bea cut in smoothly, 'I've arranged for dinner on the patio. It will be more enjoyable in the cool of the garden. Shall we go?'

They all strolled out on to the patio, Annabel still numb with shock. Yet Pierre had not turned a hair. Why should he? She had been given her congé two years ago and had been told to forget him, just as he had probably forgotten her until this unexpected meeting. He must have had scores of affairs since then. But the fact of him getting her name right proved nothing. He had the keen wit, the kind of active brain that would never get a woman's name wrong.

Until this moment Annabel had not realised how much Pierre had been in her thoughts during the last two years. All that time she had loved him, although she had not openly admitted it to herself. It was the reason new surroundings or fresh interests did nothing to soothe the whirlpool of conflicting emotions which rent her heart.

He was seated opposite to her at the table between Marilyn and her mother. Annabel sat between Bea and Dick. Once she had looked across the table to find him laughing at Marilyn's bright chatter and had caught his eye unexpectedly. She ought to have been prepared for it by now, having regard to the vow she had made never to reveal her feelings for anyone again. Yet somehow the betraying flush stained her cheeks before she had lowered her eyes on a faint smile.

For the rest of the meal, Annabel took care not to raise her eyes higher than the table and the strong sunburnt hands which had held her heart so carelessly —and still did. Some day she would have the courage to take it back.

After dinner, Marilyn suggested showing Pierre the garden. 'Aunt Bea's is much nicer than ours, and so romantic.' She had tossed a wicked glance in her mother's direction which she had deliberately ignored. But her smile at Annabel had been warm and friendly. 'Do come with us, Miss Stacey. You'll enjoy it.'

So Annabel walked with them in the country garden fresh with evening dew where flowers and small fruit trees were glimpsed among stone lanterns, twisted pines and young bamboo. Stepping stones led them to a little bridge over a stream where water trickled over stones placed with care, and Annabel recognised Aunt Bea's loving hand in the training of the flame, purple and white convolvulus supported by a wire frame.

Flowers were everywhere in the otherwise austere beauty of the Japanese garden—encouraged, of course, by Aunt Bea. Annabel had taken care to walk with Marilyn between her and Pierre. She had a strong premonition that Marilyn had wanted her company to act as a bulwark between her and Pierre, for the girl appeared to be preoccupied, with no hint of coquetry. Well, there was no cause to keep Pierre at arms' length if that was what Marilyn was doing. Pierre would never go overboard for any woman, Annabel thought.

Marilyn was saying, 'You must see Picture Island before your holiday is over. It's fabulous. There are steps everywhere, café terraces where one can dine overlooking the bay, and there are endless souvenir shops.'

'Are you staying long, Annabel?'

Pierre's deep tones struck her heart like a gong. 'About a month. It's not worth making the journey for less,' she answered coolly.

He said nothing more. Fortunately, Marilyn was never at a loss for words. She took a lively interest in the garden, commenting on strange plants and asking Pierre to explain them. He did so tolerantly, patiently, treating Marilyn as he would a child. Good heavens, surely I didn't seem a child to him too that time in Paris? Annabel found the thought disquieting. Was

23

that where she had gone wrong? Could Pierre prefer the older, more sophisticated type of woman with quick repartee? Neither she nor Marilyn qualified for that. She wondered how he had become acquainted with Marilyn and hoped for the girl's sake that she was not in love with him.

Later, when the guests had gone, Aunt Bea suggested a nightcap in the lounge before going to bed. They sat together on the settee and Bea lit a cigarette with her drink. Annabel was too tired and too dispirited to accept a cigarette. She sat sipping her drink, hoping it would eventually induce sleep.

'You look tired, my pet. I shouldn't have kept you away from your bed.'

Aunt Bea leant forward to tap off a finger of ash from her cigarette on to an ashtray on the low lacquer table and looked with concern at Annabel's drooping figure.

'I'm all right, Aunt Bea. Stop worrying,' she said, smiling convincingly. 'I love these little chats with you. Remember how we used to enjoy them at home when Granny Stacey had gone to bed?'

Bea nodded. 'By the way, Marilyn's friend was something of a surprise this evening. Quite a dish—a typical clean-shaven James Bond type. He'll fit in delightfully with a story I have in mind. You say you met him in Paris?'

'Yes. Why?'

Annabel hoped her burning cheeks would go unnoticed as she held her glass with an unsteady hand. But Bea's quick perception had noticed the strain beneath the casual question and she wondered if there had been some link between her niece's depression and the charming Pierre Devigne.

Wisely she decided that time would tell if Pierre

was staying in Japan for any length of time. She had liked him on sight and would not have said he had the look of a philanderer, although he had more than his share of devastating charm. One could never tell, of course. She said,

'Please don't think I'm probing, but do you like him?' The ensuing silence was embarrassing for both of them and she hurried on, 'Perhaps I'd better explain my reason for asking so personal a question. What do you think of the Firbanks?'

'Perfectly charming.'

'And Marilyn?'

'Quite likeable.'

Bea sighed. 'I agree. Pity she's been ruined by doting parents. Ella was married for years before she had Marilyn. Small wonder she's doted on her only child. You can imagine what she felt like when she held the child she thought she would never have in her arms for the first time.'

Bea paused at the sound of Deno locking up the house for the night, then continued:

'A year ago Marilyn became mixed up with a very undesirable pop group back in the States. They left America hurriedly after being fined heavily for drug-taking. One of them, named Kim, had a hypnotic effect upon Marilyn. He's good-looking enough if you have time to probe beneath the face fungus. Anyway, Marilyn refused to give him up and followed the group here to Japan.

'Ella and Dick were frantic and left their home and business connections in California to take a house here in order to have Marilyn with them. Wisely, they didn't try to prevent the girl from seeing this Kim provided she slept in her own bed at home each night, which the girl consented to do. While you were in the

25

garden Ella told me about Marilyn meeting Pierre at a party, and they thoroughly approved of him.

'They're now keeping their fingers crossed hoping she'll fall in love with the fascinating Pierre and so break off her association with the pop group.' Bea finished her drink and set down the glass. 'Ella has asked my help in bringing Pierre and Marilyn together. They see in Pierre the ideal partner for Marilyn, who needs an older man to be a steadying influence on her.'

Annabel also put down her drink, having lost the taste for it. It was bad enough having to meet Pierre again and hide her true feelings, but intolerable to stand by and see him hooked for the wayward Marilyn. On the other hand, Pierre had said he was not the marrying kind. She had no idea regarding his financial status and wondered if the Firbanks might be wealthy influential people who could offer him tempting bait.

'Are the Firbanks wealthy? she asked curiously.

'Practically millionaires, with interests in newspapers and shipping.'

Annabel digested this, gazing down unseeingly at the clasped hands in her lap. At last she said evenly, 'I sympathise wholeheartedly with the Firbanks and I admire them immensely for the fight they're putting up for their daughter's happiness. There would be no chance of happiness with this Kim if he's hooked on drugs. On the other hand, I don't think they should put their hopes on Pierre. He's not the marrying kind. He took great pains to acquaint me with this fact during the brief time I spent with him in Paris. Ours was a holiday interlude, nothing serious. His affair with Marilyn could end the same way.'

'Hmm,' observed Bea. 'It's quite possible for Pierre to fall in love with Marilyn. After all, he doesn't have to date her. Yet he does. I've known men to remain single for years. Then suddenly they've fallen hook, line and sinker in love—and Bob's your uncle. They've married and been ideally happy. Besides, Pierre has a lot in common with Dick Firbank, who used to be a journalist in his younger days. He might offer him a tempting job on one of his papers.'

Annabel said carefully, 'You have a point there. There is one snag. Pierre doesn't happen to be the ordinary man in the street who commutes to his office each day from nine till five. He lives dangerously and enjoys it.'

'But you would have no objection to helping us to encourage their romance?'

'Why should I?'

Bea breathed a sigh of relief. 'I'm glad. You see, the Firbanks have to return to California for a time to attend to their business commitments and I've agreed to have Marilyn stay here until they return.'

Annabel swallowed on a dry throat. 'That's nice of you.'

'Marilyn will be company for you when I'm busy writing. You won't mind going about with her, will you? She knows her way around and you're of an age to get on well together.' Bea crushed out her cigarette and smiled fondly at Annabel.

Annabel said quietly, 'I don't mind at all.'

But as she went upstairs with her aunt, she was already hating the situation she was being forced to accept. The thought of encouraging a romance between Pierre and Marilyn under the same roof with little likelihood of a respite was purgatory.

On the other hand, her aunt liked company and would be looking forward to having two young people in the house after being alone for so long.

Ashamed of her own selfish absorption in her own affairs, she kissed her aunt's cheek warmly at her bedroom door.

'Goodnight, Aunt Bea. God bless, and thanks for having me.'

Bea hugged her. 'Goodnight, my pet. Sleep well.'

Why do we Staceys have to feel things so deeply? Annabel thought as she closed the door of her room. She realised then that her aunt had not said what day Marilyn was arriving. Maybe not for a day or so, in which case she would have a little respite in which to gather her defences before meeting Pierre again. It was doubtful, though, whether it would achieve anything.

CHAPTER TWO

'I'VE an appointment with my bank manager this morning, so I suggest you come with me and we can take a look at the shops.'

Bea leaned forward to apply her lighter to Annabel's cigarette. They had breakfasted on the patio and were lingering to enjoy the early morning freshness before the heat of the day. The garden looked cool, green and fresh, and Annabel was loth to leave it.

'It's quite all right, Aunt Bea, if you have business on hand. I don't want to hold you up. I'd love to come, of course. Shopping for souvenirs is an enjoyable part of a holiday, and I know little or no Japanese.'

A shadow passed quickly over her face as she remembered shopping with Pierre in Paris.

Bea, noting the shadow, wondered what had put it

there. 'You're not worrying about the earthquakes we have here, are you, my pet?'

Annabel looked startled. 'Goodness, no. How bad are they?'

Bea shrugged philosophically. 'One becomes accustomed to them, like the shedding of shoes when one enters a building.' Her eyes twinkled. 'I was terrified at first. Fortunately we're fairly safe here. The greatest hazard is fire. Scared?'

Annabel shook her head. 'No. I'm going to love it here. It's so refreshingly different from anything I've ever seen before.' She leaned back in her chair with a sigh of deep contentment as bells tinkled across the bay from some shrine. 'Nothing is perfect, is it? There's always something to contend with abroad—snakes, typhoons or droughts,' she said wistfully.

Deno strode on the patio in that moment before Bea could answer. He carried a bouquet of white roses, young buds with the dew still fresh on them, and with a beaming face presented them to Annabel.

'For me?' she gasped.

The colour flooded her face when she found Pierre's card attached to the delicate fern. It had not receded when Deno took the flowers away to put them in water.

'As I said before,' Bea commented dryly as she tapped ash from her cigarette on to an ashtray on the table, 'that young man is going to provide splendid copy for my new book. By the way, I have two cars in the garage. You can use them at any time. The big one is the best, because the roads are dreadfully marred by potholes. Marilyn has a big car which she'll bring with her when she comes.'

'When is she coming?'

'Any time now. Her room is ready. You need have

29

no fear of going about with her. She's a competent driver.'

The subject of Marilyn came up again when they were on their way to Tokyo in Bea's big car.

She observed airily, 'Marilyn is an enigma—quite brainy, she did well at university, yet so naïve and useless. Pity she has an unlimited income. Without it, she might have carved out a useful career for herself.'

'Could her wealth be the reason the pop group are hovering around the honeypot?' Annabel murmured thoughtfully.

'Could be.'

Bea concentrated on her driving, for they were approaching the city. The heat of the car made Annabel steam and she removed her sunglasses. The city bulged on all sides with traffic, pedestrians and advertisements. Gaudy banners waved and dangled from roofs and buildings like giant leaflets dropped indiscriminately by a helicopter, defying one to ignore them. Ginza Street positively burst with them at the seams, overflowing into narrow side roads and between bridges.

Bea parked the car in a small cobbled courtyard behind a corner book shop.

'I always park here,' she said. 'The proprietor of the bookshop is a friend of mine. Perhaps you'd like to go in and look around while I go along to the bank. It isn't far away. Just down the road.'

Annabel had put on her sunglasses and walked from the bright sunlight into the dim little shop. The little proprietor came from the shadows to greet her with a smile which showed more gold teeth than white, accompanied by a courteous bow.

There was a good selection of English, American and Japanese literature and good class magazines.

Annabel bought several books, including one by Lafcadio Hearn, and the proprietor was parcelling them up when she noticed a stand beside the counter displaying Aunt Bea's latest crime novel. There was a good photograph of her on the top of the display.

'Would Miss Stacey autograph one or two of her books for me to send to my friends at home, Annabel?'

Startled by the familiar deep tones, she swung round to gaze up into Pierre's dark teasing eyes. He looked immaculate in a cream linen suit, was hatless and wore sunglasses too. As usual he was his elegant self, lean and uncaring.

Annabel's heart gave a painful jolt. 'She'll be delighted and thrilled, especially if you give them to her yourself.'

He smiled down at her. Then turning to the stand he presented wide, strong shoulders while he selected several of Bea's books including earlier editions from a pile near by. He waited while Annabel paid for and received her parcel of books before handing his over to the shopkeeper.

Still smiling, he said, 'You have not come to town alone, have you?'

She shook her head and told him about Bea going to the bank.

'I will walk down with you to the bank, if I may. I would like to hear what you have been doing in the last two years.'

He went with her to the car where she left her parcel before strolling with him along the street. Her thoughts were mixed when several times she was forced to move near to him by the jostling crowds. Yet, despite the turmoil inside her, her voice was even enough when she told him about her work, ending

31

with Grandmother Stacey's death and Aunt Bea's entrance into the world of writers.

Pieerre listened intently and, in turn, told her a little of the places he had been to. His deep tone was non-committal, impersonal in a way, to discourage any probing.

Annabel wondered if he was going to see Marilyn and would have liked to know how often they met.

Casually she enquired, 'How long are you staying in Tokyo? Are you on another assignment or in between them?'

They had reached the bank entrance when he replied:

'A bit of both,' dryly.

He drew her close as a dog, obviously feeling the heat, dashed by madly between moving feet. The feel of his hard lean body against her own for those few palpitating seconds before he partially released her increased the nervous tension building up inside her. So close, yet poles apart, for he was not the Pierre she had known in Paris. This man seemed older and a little more grim.

Annabel swallowed on an aching void of love and despair drying her throat and pricking the back of her eyes. Looking up at him across the aching void of the past two years, she saw him as he had wanted her to, as a man who had grown accustomed to becoming a loner, a man who would strain against the bonds of matrimony until they snapped.

He was smiling down at her, a smile that allured and startled making her heart beat alarmingly fast.

She said hurriedly, 'Thanks for the roses. They're beautiful, and it was very nice of you to send them.'

His smile bantered. 'I bet you have had lots of flowers from admirers.'

She lifted her chin. 'Probably as many as you've sent to the ladies of your acquaintance.'

He let this pass, still holding her a little protectively against the crowds passing. 'I imagined you spending your holiday with your parents in Paris. You did not go last year?'

'No. I went to Spain with a friend.'

'And no Paris again this year? What do your parents say about that?'

'Aunt Bea wanted me to come and stay with her. We haven't seen each other for two years.'

'Do you like it here?'

He kept a steady hold on her arm and Annabel blessed the sunglasses hiding the pain in her eyes. How she longed to tell him that it was heaven with him beside her.

'Very much,' she answered steadily.

Several people were leaving the bank, among them Bea.

Pierre said, 'There's your aunt. I'll be going. *Au revoir*, see you soon.'

Numbly, Annabel watched him stride away, longing to call him back.

'Wasn't that the charming Pierre?' Aunt Bea asked, lifting arched brows. 'I hope I didn't scare him away.'

'Pierre doesn't scare easily.' Annabel told her about the books he wanted autographed, and about their meeting in the bookshop.

They were on their way home when Annabel saw Marilyn. She was emerging from a side street in a rather dreary quarter of the town. A rather disreputable young man in jeans and a soiled white shirt minus a tie walked with her. His long hair, straggling to his shoulders, was confused with the wild growth of beard on his face. He was slouching along with a cigarette dangling from his mouth listening to Marilyn, who was talking to him urgently. Then she looked up and saw Annabel.

She lifted a hand, but Marilyn did nothing. She just stared until the car had passed. Bea had been too engrossed with her driving to notice, and Annabel decided to say nothing. She was not narrow-minded, but the sight of a well-educated and sophisticated young woman associating with a hippy nauseated her. Was her companion the Kim Aunt Bea had mentioned?

Annabel suppressed a shudder. Whoever it was Marilyn had to be saved from herself. She wanted to help but had no idea what she could do. Her sympathy was with Marilyn's parents.

After lunch, Aunt Bea went to her study to look out some bonds for her bank manager and Annabel went upstairs to her room. Putting away the presents she had bought turned her thoughts once again to Marilyn.

Aunt Bea was certainly taking on a responsibility in having the girl stay with her while her parents were away. No doubt the Firbanks were easier in their minds because they had left their daughter in the care of Miss Stacey and her niece. While it was nice to have a companion of her own age, Annabel doubted whether Marilyn and herself had much in common. She would have much preferred to have been alone with her aunt than to have a third person present.

After all, they were family and the American girl was a complete outsider. Furthermore, she was a friend of Pierre, which meant she would meet him often when she wanted to avoid him. The old pain stabbed at her heart at the thought of him. Did he know about Marilyn's affair with Kim? Annabel thought not. Anyway, it was no affair of hers. Pierre could take care of himself. Even so, she could not rest.

She was on her way downstairs again when the phone rang in the hall. It was Ella Firbank. They were about to start out to catch their plane to the States and were calling to drop Marilyn's cases on the way. Marilyn had gone on ahead to do a little last-minute shopping for them in Tokyo. She was to say goodbye to them from there.

Annabel went in search of Aunt Bea and they were waiting at the front door when the Firbanks arrived. Deno carried Marilyn's cases from the car and Ella Firbank reiterated her gratitude.

'We don't know how to thank you,' she told Bea shakily, with a wavering smile for Annabel. It was obvious that they were both upset and shaken at the thought of leaving Marilyn. 'You see, apart from Dick, Marilyn is all I have. I do hope we're doing the right thing in leaving her.'

Bea said reassuringly, 'Now don't you worry. We shall see she's all right. Like you,' kindly, 'I believe in giving her a free hand. Any interference would only send her off to join the group. On the other hand, I don't think she'll do anything silly.'

Annabel, cutting flowers from the garden for Marilyn's room, wondered if the Firbanks were fighting a losing battle where their daughter was concerned. The girl had been pampered and petted and every whim gratified until out of sheer boredom she had escaped via Kim and his group.

On the other hand, what she felt for Kim could be hero-worship. If that was the case then what she felt for him was not love but infatuation. And there was hope for her. Unless she had also been hooked on drugs. Annabel shuddered, hoping with all her heart that this was not the case.

Marilyn came after dinner that evening with the excuse that she had been leaving things shipshape at home. The house was to be locked up while her parents were away and the staff were taking a holiday.

On arriving, she went to her room and did not appear again. Annabel had the feeling that the grey-green eyes avoided her own and in that moment she had wished Marilyn and her troubles miles away. She had been looking forward to this holiday so much with Aunt Bea. Now it was all spoiled.

After an early morning swim in the bay the next morning, Annabel had breakfast with Aunt Bea on the patio. Marilyn had not put in an appearance when, later, Bea went to her study to check the proofs of her last novel in order to return it to her publisher. It was half past ten when Annabel went along to Marilyn's room, to find her in bed.

She looked very pretty in a white frothy lace and beribboned nightgress. Her yellow hair was sprayed over the pillow like rays from the morning sun and she blinked wary grey-green eyes at Annabel, who was looking fresh and sweet in lettuce green linen.

Annabel smiled as she entered the room. 'Good morning, Marilyn. I hope I'm not intruding, but it's such a beautiful day and I wondered if you'd care to go for a walk or a drive later.' Her small laugh was meant to be apologetic. 'Aunt Bea is tied up with her work and I'm at a loose end myself. I thought we could talk together by way of a beginning. We ought to have quite an assortment of topics to discuss since we know so little about each other.'

She walked to the window and drew the curtains, turning to see Marilyn pushing herself up in bed to stretch her shapely arms above her head and yawn luxuriously. To Annabel's sensitive ears the yawn was mixed with a sigh of relief. Uncomfortably, it occurred to her then that Marilyn probably thought she had told her aunt about seeing her the previous day and that they had been discussing her.

Marilyn swung long legs out of bed, thrust her feet in white fur mules and reached out a pink-tipped hand for the matching negligée thrown over the back of a chair. Shrugging into it, she said awkwardly, 'I'm sorry about yesterday. For staring at you so blankly, I mean. I didn't expect to see you and—well, the car shot by so quickly, didn't it?'

'Yes, it did, and Aunt Bea was too busy with the traffic to notice you.' The atmosphere, frayed with undercurrent, forced Annabel to go on. 'I didn't tell Aunt Bea I'd seen you.'

Marilyn stood up and shook her yellow hair back from her face almost defiantly. The grey-green eyes glittered flintily.

'I suppose you know all about me.'

Annabel met her gaze openly. 'I know about you and Kim—Aunt Bea told me a little when she said you were coming here to stay. I hope you don't mind.'

'I suppose you're shocked.'

Annabel laughed. 'One isn't shocked easily these days. I must confess, though, that I was surprised to see you in such company. It wasn't the real you, somehow.'

Marilyn lifted a hand to study her nails. 'Perhaps I'm two persons, one fighting the other.'

'Aren't we all? Was that Kim you were with yesterday?' lightly.

'No, that was Don. Kim isn't well. I'm worried about him.'

Annabel thrust her hands into the large patch pockets of the green linen. She felt no desire to be drawn into the mess Marilyn was making of her life. And yet any call for help, and the girl did need help, always touched a vulnerable spot. At last she spoke in a voice which held the right degree of ordinary interest.

'Suppose you get dressed and have breakfast, then afterwards, we can take a little stroll down to the beach. I'd like to help if I can and I promise to treat everything you care to tell me in confidence. However, I want you to know that my sympathy is all for your parents. They're two nice people and I'd hate to see them hurt.'

Later, when they walked down to the little secluded bay, Marilyn told how she had first met Kim and the group. By an odd twist of fate, her parents had engaged the group to play at her twenty-first birthday party. Marilyn had fallen for Kim on sight. He had been no drug addict then, but success had come too soon and he had taken drugs in order to keep up his vitality for the endless engagements the group filled all over the country.

Kim came from a very good family and had formed the group while still at college. He had been twenty-one when he had been fined for possessing drugs. They had been filling a long-term engagement in Japan when Kim had been taken ill. Marilyn had followed them there and had nursed Kim until he was well again. The group liked life in Japan and now had a permanent booking at a night club.

Annabel had listened intently to the whole story. They had reached the beach and were sitting down on the sand gazing across the sparkling water.

'Are you going to marry Kim?' she asked.

Marilyn took in a rasping breath. 'I don't know.'

'You mean he hasn't asked you or you aren't sure of

your own feelings towards him?'

'He hasn't asked me.'

'It couldn't be infatuation, this thing you feel for him?'

Marilyn shook her head and looked utterly dejected. 'I don't know. All I know is I just couldn't abandon him if I wanted to. Don't ask me why.'

Annabel thought of her own love for Pierre. What a sorry pair they were—both of them in love with a man they would never have. The heat from the sun grew more intense as the midday hour approached.

Restlessly, she rose to her feet. 'Come on, let's paddle along the beach in the water. It's quite hot. We ought to have brought our swim-suits.'

Slipping off her sandals, Annabel carried them and began to wade through the cool water.

Marilyn followed suit. 'So you met Pierre in Paris two years ago,' she said more in a relaxed frame of mind. 'He isn't married, is he? He says not.'

'No, he's not married. Pierre isn't the marrying kind.'

Marilyn laughed. 'All men are the marrying kind if a woman goes the right way about it!'

'Is that how you feel about Kim?'

'Yes. But Kim is losing his looks. He used to be so handsome—not as virile as Pierre nor so masculine. Kim is someone you have to mother. Pierre is someone who would look after you. He's so male in an exciting kind of way. It's hard to believe he isn't married.'

'I agree. It's one thing to hook a man and quite another to keep him on the hook.'

'I see what you mean. A lot depends upon the bait, though, doesn't it?' Marilyn gave a small rueful laugh. 'I'm not so dumb as not to be aware of the fact that I could be wooed for my fortune.' She thrust an arm through Annabel's and her laugh this time was more of a chuckle. 'Do you know, I've just discovered something. I don't think I would mind being married for my money if it was someone like Pierre, for instance. He's such a dishy guy that a girl would be happy to have him on any terms.'

They returned hot and sticky to the house to find Aunt Bea seated on the patio with a cool drink. She looked cool and relaxed in a lemon trouser suit.

She said, 'You look hot, my dears. Come, sit down and have an iced drink before lunch.'

Lunch was an extremely pleasant meal with all three women utterly relaxed. When it was over they lingered with cigarettes watching brightly winged birds swooping down for crumbs.

'What have you two girls in mind for this afternoon? It's really too hot to do anything strenuous.'

Aunt Bea smiled fondly on them both and Marilyn shook her head.

'Count me out of your plans. Pierre is calling for me this afternoon,' she informed them.

'I'll probably take a book and go down to the beach again,' Annabel said.

Suddenly the next few moments were all confusion as the biggest spider Annabel had ever seen crawled on to her plate at the table. With a shriek she leapt to her feet and took to her heels.

She had not gone far before she cannoned into something solid striding in her direction between the flower beds. Strong arms whipped round her.

'Easy now,' Pierre said softly, drawing her trembling figure against him. 'What happened?'

He looked over her head at Marilyn, who sat convulsed with laughter.

'Oh dear!' she gasped, wiping tears of mirth from her eyes. 'It was so funny!'

Aunt Bea was very concerned. 'Are you all right, Annabel? It's quite harmless.'

But Annabel was clinging to Pierre's tailored continental shirt which he wore with a silk cravat tucked in at the neck opening. He was minus a jacket. Still trembling, she wanted Marilyn and Bea to go away and leave her in the lovely Japanese garden in Pierre's arms. She almost blessed the spider, frightening though it was, for catapulting her into his arms.

Lifting her eyes not higher than his strong brown throat, she said,

'I'm sorry for being such a coward, but it was such a huge spider. And ... and it startled me.'

Pierre released her to place a brotherly arm around her slim shoulders as they walked back to the table. 'Don't apologise for being startled,' he said.

'I'm sorry.' Bea looked very apologetic. 'I should have warned you about our uninvited guest who comes each day for crumbs. Deno has christened him Mariko, which means Little Ball. When he's eaten, he curls himself up into a ball and goes to sleep!'

But Annabel only half heard. She was thinking that nothing had changed between herself and Pierre. Even a lovesick fool like herself could not find the slightest trace of love in the way he had held her against him.

Marilyn, leaning forward in her chair to stub out the last of her cigarette, reached out to pick up Annabel's sunglasses from the table.

'Your sunglasses, Annabel. You'll need them this afternoon on the beach.' Somewhat carelessly she then turned to Pierre, who had kept his arm around Annabel's shoulders. 'Annabel is spending the afternoon on the beach with a book.'

'Thanks.'

Annabel took the sunglasses, stifling an impulse to stiffen against Pierre's hold on her shoulders.

'I think she'd better come along with us.' He was smiling down at Annabel, lean, brown, mocking and undeniably attractive. His shoulders were wide and strong in the tailored shirt. He had the congenital gift of looking correct in everything he wore. 'Mariko, the spider, has taken a fancy to you, *chérie*, and will not be within following you down to the beach.'

Marilyn rose from her chair. 'Stop teasing her, Pierre. She can come with us if she wants to.'

'She is coming.' Pierre's voice held a note of finality.

CHAPTER THREE

PIERRE'S car, a scarlet Jaguar racer, took the three of them comfortably in the front seat. Annabel sat in the middle. She felt the hard leanness of his body against her and his brown flexible fingers on the wheel of the car drew her eyes like a magnet.

The car roared along, creating a refreshing breeze which ruffled their bare heads and tempered the heat of the sun blazing down on them. They had reached the Imperial Hotel when Marilyn said, 'Drop me off here, Pierre. I want to ring up the airport to see if Interflora have delivered the flowers I've sent for Mother on her arrival in the States. I shall probably be a while putting the call through, so I'll meet you both later in the park.'

Annabel thought Marilyn's request rather odd, since she could easily have rung up before she left Aunt

Bea's. It was obvious she had other plans in mind. Pierre, however, dropped her off unperturbed.

The park near by was a charmingly beautiful land-scaped garden, an oasis in the heart of the city enclosing a lake. Stepping stones meandered along grassy paths and across streams and there were captivating old thatched summerhouses where one could partake of refreshment and watch the pretty kimonoed girls walk by.

Pierre parked the car and Annabel strolled beside him, wanting to hang on to each precious minute of time. At close quarters he was overwhelming and she began to wonder whether she had been wise to come. Then gradually she began to relax and looked around her with an eager interest as she listened to the deep voice of her companion.

Like her, Pierre enjoyed Japan and felt curiously at home. He shared her interest in the people, also, understanding by instinct their simple way of life, their simple joys and their many hardships and sorrows.

Apart from his directness and honesty which made such an overwhelming appeal to her sensitive nature, Annabel wondered what it was about Pierre which made him so irresistible to women. He was *le plus dangereux des hommes* who never committed himself, and the strongness of his appeal lay in the fact that he was chock full of the vitality of a very male person.

As they approached a curly-roofed pagoda next to a summerhouse, Pierre said, 'The pagoda is meant as a place in which to meditate and purify the mind before entering the teahouse. The tea ceremony originated centuries ago by Buddhist monks who drank green tea to keep them awake during the long hours of prayer and meditation. Shall we go in the teahouse?'

They shed their shoes at the door of the teahouse to walk along polished floors of delicately scented sandalwood to a room with a finely carved ceiling. Spotless tatami mats in soft shades of green and yellow covered the polished wooden floor, blending with the gardens which seemed to spill inside through the open aperture of sliding glass windows.

It was cool as they sat on their heels beneath overhead fans on the tatami matting to face a young monk in a black kimono. The tea was made by boiling a kettle on a charcoal brazier in front of him and the water poured on to green powdered tea in small handleless bowls. The tea was then whisked around with a bamboo brush, turned twice slowly in the left hand and then offered to a guest. The guest then turned it round twice before drinking it.

Pierre was offered the first bowl of tea, for men took precedence over women in Japan. Tiny rice cakes on leaves were offered with it. When the ceremony was over, Annabel clutched Pierre's hand as she straightened her cramped legs painfully from the unaccustomed kneeling.

'Enjoy it?' he asked, bending down at the door to put on her shoes.

'Very much,' she replied.

There was still no sign of Marilyn when they strolled back to the car. They sat in the car within sight of the park entrance and Pierre narrowed a gaze at the people entering. Annabel said nothing. She was not sure if he knew about Marilyn's association with Kim and his group and it was none of her business to enlighten him. She had given her word to treat everything Marilyn had told her in confidence.

Pierre took out cigarettes and offered them. When Annabel refused, he lighted one for himself and said casually, 'Marilyn smokes her head off.'

'Probably a bit highly strung. She's a nice person, though.'

Annabel wondered why she was carrying a torch for her obvious rival.

'A charming family,' was the cool comment. 'No less charming than your own.' He went on to ask about her parents. He had been home to Paris only once during the past two years. 'I found it haunted,' he said, blowing out a line of smoke through the car window.

She looked at him wide-eyed. 'Haunted?' she echoed.

He turned his head and smiled down at her, the slow charming smile that always made her feel curiously weak.

'Yes, *chérie*. Haunted by a small face with brimming blue eyes eloquent with love.'

Annabel stiffened as his hand covered the small one in her lap. She drew hers away as if it had been stung, for it seemed to her then how infinitely more empty her life would be when they parted for a second time. How was she going to bear it? She had to. There was no alternative. Her line of thought was leading to self-pity—a disastrous course.

The bitter emptiness of the last two years without him welled up in her throat, threatening to choke her. This time she would be the one to give him his *congé*, treat him as he had treated her. He would not suffer the torment she had suffered when he had done the same to her because he was not in love with her. It was the only way, a kind of self-defence against a second crushing blow.

Her smile was as mocking as she could make it, her voice perfectly steady.

'If you're referring to my foolishness of two years ago, forget it. The calf love I felt for you was in the process of my growing up. If I appear in the least disturbed when I'm with you put it down to embarrassment. No woman likes to be reminded of the time she made a fool of herself.'

Her eyes flayed his. Self-disgust blazed in them, fighting her fear of capitulating to his charm—to her love for him.

For several moments he stared at her curiously, sadly.

'*Vraiment, cher enfant,*' he murmured at last. 'Did I do that to you? I cannot put into words...'

Annabel stopped him abruptly with a wave of her hand. Wave after wave of emotion washed over her as she kept her eyes on his face, his dark controlled expressionless face. Pain laid deep shadows in her quiet eyes. How dared he use that half caressing tone as if ... as if she was the same little idiot whom he had charmed two years ago?

'Forget it,' she cried wildly. 'This is most embarrassing to me, since I'm more or less engaged to someone else.'

Annabel spoke the fatal words, looking stonily ahead, seeing yet not seeing the wedding car draw up at the entrance to the Imperial Hotel across the road to deposit a newly married Japanese couple evidently attending their wedding reception.

The dainty little bride with her black, lacquered, elaborate hair covered by the traditional white satin hat, her beautiful kimono and fabulous obi around her tiny waist, hardly registered on Annabel's unhappy brain.

She glanced at Pierre's hands resting quietly on the car wheel with the cigarette smouldering between his fingers. He sat motionless, not a whit put out by her dramatic announcement. Why should he show any emotion? Te had not shown any two years ago, so why now?

'Someone you have known a long time?' he asked.

'Not too long. He's a Q. C.'

'Hello.' Suddenly Marilyn was there, her golden hair a halo for the bright smile. 'I've been doing one or two errands.'

She slipped into her seat beside Annabel and Pierre set the car in motion.

That evening, dressing for dinner, Annabel had still not recovered from her outburst to Pierre when she had hinted at a possible engagement. While she had spoken the truth she knew she had hinted at something that would never happen.

The man in question, Francis Kerrison, Q. C., worked at chambers adjoining the office where she was employed as an accountant. He was thirty-five, handsome and all set for a brilliant career at the Bar. He had also asked her repeatedly to marry him. Funnily enough, they had met on the plane in which Annabel had been returning from Paris.

Her heart, freshly bruised by Pierre, had been susceptible to his frank appraisal. He was sternly good-looking with a sardonic sense of humour. It had seemed like fate that she should eventually work in an office near to his chambers. They had met accidentally, sometimes on her way to the office, and he had given her a lift in his fabulous car. The casual dinner date had become a regular one, and Annabel became gradually convinced that Francis Kerrison was the only man who could help her forget Pierre.

She knew now that she had merely been deluding

47

herself. The moment she had met Pierre, Annabel knew there could never be anyone else to replace him in her affections. The sound of a car arriving drew her to the window to look down below where Pierre, armed with the parcel of books to be autographed and a bouquet of flowers for his hostess, strode to the door.

There had been four of them for dinner, Aunt Bea, Marilyn, Pierre and Annabel. They had coffee on the patio sitting in a cosy semi-circle overlooking the garden. Dinner had been an enjoyable meal with Marilyn happy to be away from the constant surveillance of fond parents. Pierre had been his usual charming self. He had a rare and happy combination of audacity and courtesy which added to his charm and which seized and held the attention of his companions.

Annabel had found it utterly impossible to remain immune from his personality. He drew her with a fatal magnetism like a poor defenceless pin to the steel of his charm. Even Aunt Bea had hung on to his every word and had obviously been completely captivated by the man.

Yet, during the meal, her spirits had risen in an atmosphere of lighthearted laughter and chatter until all things unpleasant had been forgotten. Pierre's flowers formed an attractive centrepiece for the table, exuding a pleasing fragrance on which Annabel concentrated sooner than meet his sardonic gaze.

Suddenly there were firm footsteps on the garden path. Someone had apparently arrived by car and, on hearing their voices, had made their way through the garden to the patio.

The man who rounded the corner of the house was of medium height, an athletic middle-aged man with a boyish smile. He confronted them, smiling first at Bea then, with a faint apologetic expression, at her guests.

Bea rose to her feet. 'John! How nice of you to call.'

He came forward. 'I meant to meet you yesterday when you arrived, but couldn't make it. Welcome back. Did you have a nice holiday?'

'Lovely, thanks. Do sit down. Have you dined?' Bea pulled up a chair beside her.

'Thanks.' He hitched up the immaculate trousers of his evening suit and sat down to join them as they sat facing the garden. 'I've dined at my club. I have news for you. At two o'clock this morning I became a grandfather after sitting glued to the phone for more hours than I care to remember.'

Bea chuckled. 'Good for you! A grandson, I hope, who'll be called John?' When he nodded she spoke to Deno, who was clearing the table. 'Champagne, please, Deno. This calls for a celebration. How is Claire?'

'Fine after a rough time. She has taken it badly that her mother will never see the baby.'

'Of course.' Bea's voice was gentle and her colour, which had deepened upon his appearance, went back to normal. 'John, may I present my niece, Annabel, Miss Marilyn Firbank and Monsieur Pierre Devigne. Sir John Lakerwood.'

John leaned forward to shake hands with Annabel, seated next to her aunt, then Marilyn and Pierre.

'So you're now a grandfather. How does it feel?' Aunt Bea teased.

John chuckled. 'All of my fifty years.'

Annabel, noticing her aunt's flushed cheeks when the man had arrived, scented a romance. She looked with interest at the twinkling grey eyes and white wings of hair at his temples.

'You don't look old enough to be a grandfather,' she assured him. 'Men who don't lose their hair seldom

49

do. Don't you agree, Aunt Bea?'

Bea laughed and coloured again quite charmingly. 'I do indeed. Like good cognac, John, like Pierre, will improve with age.'

John leaned forward to address Pierre. 'That last remark from our charming hostess makes us brothers, so to speak. Excuse me for asking, but aren't you the journalist chap who wrote that very interesting article about world finance in a recent issue of the *Kyoto Shimnon*?'

Pierre nodded and their conversation was interrupted by the appearance of Deno with a bottle of champagne and glasses on a tray. The toast to the new baby was drunk and conversation began anew. Marilyn was the first to excuse herself and go to her room, saying she was tired after a hectic week of late nights. Pierre was the next to make a move and Annabel went with him to his car.

With his hands thrust into his pockets, Pierre strolled nonchalantly beside her. His strong tanned profile looked stern. His thoughts, Annabel felt, were miles away.

At last he said, 'I was not in the least bit interested in coming to Japan. I have been to so many places that another, more or less, did not make much difference. How often does it happen that we look forward to a trip only to be disappointed at the end of it. Whereas we set off on a trip on which we could not care less and find its magic colouring our whole life.'

Thinking he was referring to his meeting with Marilyn, Annabel said carefully, 'You've been very fortunate in being born and brought up in enchanting Paris. Everywhere else compares unfavourably with it to one who loves it as you do.'

'Ah, Paris!' He gave a very French shrug.

'But you adore Paris. You told me you would never wish to settle anywhere else.'

They had reached his car and he looked down into her eyes with a curious expression.

'So I do. You were there. Remember?'

Remember! Would to heaven she could forget. He would never know what her smile cost her.

'I'm here too.'

He said deliberately, 'I imagined to find you changed in two years. Yet I find you the same sweet and innocent child who still believes in all the love duets your parents sing.'

She said hotly, 'And why not? My parents are happy together and will always love each other as they did when they were married.'

He considered for a moment. 'Always is a long time. I know that you are the faithful kind, but will the man you marry be the same? Will he come up to your expectations?'

Annabel looked away from his dark intent gaze to the changing shadows across the garden merging with those of the distant hills. She was sorely tempted to tell him she was not committed to any engagement with any man, but somehow the words would not come. Instead, she turned and looked up into his face.

'He's English with the same ideals as myself. I would say we have a good chance of happiness together.'

He was leaning back now against the car and something strange in his attitude—surely it could not be dejection?—stirred her oddly. Her whole soul was drawn towards him. She was on the brink of throwing herself into his arms, a move that would probably have changed the whole course of their lives, when a slow ominous rumbling at their feet struck terror in

51

her heart.

The earth rocked crazily. Yet there was no wind.

'Oh!' she cried, looking up at him with the wide-eyed stare of a bewildered child. 'Oh!' she repeated as the dreadful upheaval increased.

Pierre drew her into his arms and laid his cheek to her hair.

'Stop trembling, *chérie*,' he murmured gently yet with authority. 'Just stand quietly until it passes. I have you safe.'

Annabel tried to break away, preferring the unknown terror to the sweet torture of his embrace. 'But Aunt Bea ... the house?'

'The house will stand. It is built on rock and Sir John is with your aunt, so do not worry, *mon enfant*.'

To Annabel the following nightmare minutes were an eternity. She was trembling herself. Now, with his arms around her, she grew calmer. The closeness of his hard lean frame against her was sending vibrating rays through her whole being and setting unknown little sparks alight. The perfume of the night was all around them and his arms were lifting her up above the frightening noise and jigging of a world suddenly gone mad.

Clinging to him, her face buried in his chest, she was not afraid. How could she be in his beloved arms? The agony was bitter-sweet. Soon the tremors would cease and Pierre would take his leave. Had the earth opened in that moment to swallow them up she would have welcomed it, clasped closely as she was in his embrace.

The relief from the noise when the tremors ended was overwhelming. They stood for endless seconds in silence. It was then Annabel realised that Pierre had drawn her closer with a suffocating tightness.

He was speaking in her hair and the fact that his voice sounded unlike him was another crazy delusion of a crazy interlude. 'It is over, *mignonne*. There is nothing to fear. You have had your first earthquake.'

Slowly she looked up at him. Pale as a magnolia, she drew herself away from arms which no longer compelled. Their eyes met and clung, hungry with emptiness. Aunt Bea broke the spell.

'Annabel, Pierre, where are you?

The next moment she was there with Sir John. Behind them, the house slumbered on as though it had never been disturbed from its sleep. Annabel said lightly, 'We're all right. What about Marilyn? Do you think she was scared?'

Bea shrugged. 'Like me, Marilyn is used to them. I'll go up to see how she is. Meanwhile, suppose we all go to the lounge for a last drink.'

Prompted by some strange impulse, Annabel said, 'I'll go.'

She moved swiftly towards the house, wondering with despair which of them would be the first to leave Japan. Pierre or herself? She hoped she would be the first. It would be balm to her sore heart to feel that she was the one walking out.

The peal of a fire engine pierced the night air, growing louder, then fading away in the distance. She hoped no one had been killed. Some of the very old buildings had looked very unstable. She shuddered and stopped at Marilyn's door.

Her room was as silent as a tomb. Marilyn had complained of feeling tired and had probably slept through it all. Annabel tapped gently on the door. When her second tap received no reply, she opened the door very quietly. Silence met her, the profound silence of an empty room.

'Marilyn,' she whispered, not wishing to waken her if she was asleep. 'Marilyn,' she repeated.

The untouched bed looked serene and dreamy in the moonlight streaming through the window. She walked to the window. Far away in the town she glimpsed the glow of a distant fire—only a small one. There was no sign of destruction as far as she could make out in the gloom.

A swift glance in the bathroom told her Marilyn was not there. Nor was she anywhere in the house. And yet she could not have left in her car without them being aware of it. The only other answer was that someone had picked her up at the end of the lane. Kim, of course.

Annabel's first reaction was one of anger against Marilyn for behaving so underhandedly in Aunt Bea's house. What an idiot the girl was! And yet even as her anger rose it subsided. Her small face softened. One did crazy things when one was in love.

The problem was what was she to say when she returned downstairs to Aunt Bea. Ask Pierre to look for Marilyn? Telling Pierre would mean mentioning Kim, because she would have to tell Pierre where she thought Marilyn was. She could not do that. Besides, Aunt Bea would be dreadfully worried until the girl was found.

She would say nothing and trust to luck that the wretched girl came back unharmed. After all, she seemed perfectly capable of taking care of herself. Closing Marilyn's door, Annabel went swiftly downstairs.

Pierre met her in the hall. 'How is she?' he asked.

'Out like a light.' Cheered that there was some truth in her statement, Annabel went on. 'I hope I can sleep as soundly through the next earthquake!'

They strolled outside to his car. Bea was lower down the drive with Sir John.

Pierre said urgently, 'Dine with me tomorrow evening, Annabel.'

He had taken her hand and she tried to withdraw it—to no avail.

'I don't know what arrangements Aunt Bea has made,' she said feebly.

'She is dining with Sir John,' grimly.

'There's Marilyn too ... I don't know ...'

He looked down at her with disconcerting dark eyes. 'Thursday, then. You have three days' notice.' He kissed her hand before releasing it. Then, raising his voice a fraction, he said, 'Goodnight, Miss Stacey. Thanks for a pleasant evening and for autographing the books. Goodnight, Sir John, Annabel.'

Annabel inclined her head to his mocking salute and the next moment he was in his car and roaring away into the night.

'Well, how was Marilyn?'

John had gone and Bea linked Annabel's arm as they walked back to the house.

'Out like a light,' which in a way was quite true, thought Annabel wryly.

CHAPTER FOUR

THE pearly grey morning sallied forth with the promise of yet another fine day, giving no indication of the tremors of the previous evening. Slowly the sun rose above the grey film of cloud to disperse the scarves of mist drifting around the mountain peaks.

Annabel, going down to the beach before breakfast

for an early bathe, viewed the brilliance of the blue and gold day with an ache in her heart. The beauty of her surroundings mocked at her and she found herself resenting the intrusion of Marilyn and Pierre to ruin the holiday she had so looked forward to.

She had lain awake the previous evening waiting for Marilyn to return. Her quick ears had caught the sound of her furtive entry about three o'clock in the morning.

Deno had returned soon after. He was a member of a voluntary force who turned out after an earthquake to help if needed. With Marilyn disposed of, Annabel had been a long time in going off to sleep, thinking about Pierre.

Already she was beginning to understand the kind of self-suppression she would have to practise in her love for him. For Pierre, life held no problems. His way of life offered a continuity of change and action, a feeling of always moving on to some fresh interest.

Meeting him again had awakened her need of him. She wanted him with every beat of her heart. So Annabel had at last fallen asleep still fighting her battle, praying for common sense to prevail over unrequited love.

The bay was deserted and she swam leisurely in the cool water, enjoying the solitude. On her way back to the house she wondered if Aunt Bea would be up to have breakfast with her. She had not the taste for her own company these days. A companion to talk to kept one from thinking.

'Good morning, my pet. Enjoy your bathe?'

Aunt Bea met her in the hall and Annabel leaned forward to kiss her cheek.

'It was lovely.'

'Good. I thought you would have been lying in this

morning to catch up on your sleep. Don't go up to change. Deno has gone to fetch your breakfast. He saw you coming through the garden. I'm sure your swim has given you an appetite.'

They went to the dining room and Annabel found that she was ready for her breakfast. It was like old times, just Aunt Bea and herself talking about people and places they both knew. The chief topic of conversation was the earthquake.

Bea said on a reminiscent shudder, 'The thing that really scares me is the fact that while we're comparatively safe here other people might not be so lucky. And there's nothing we can do about it.'

Annabel nodded, spreading marmalade on her toast. 'Did Deno say if there were any casualties?'

'One or two old buildings near the Ginza collapsed, but there were no casualties.' Bea replenished their coffee cups. 'Thank heaven for Deno! He's a pillar of strength on such occasions. An earthquake is as natural to him as a shower of rain. His utter calm and reassuring smile make me feel ashamed of quaking myself. I pretended to be so calm and collected in front of John.' She smiled and her eyes twinkled. 'He wasn't very impressed.'

'I'm sure he was,' Annabel spoke with conviction. 'Neither you nor Sir John would be lacking in courage in times of stress.'

'You're right about John. As for me,' ruefully, 'I was thankful for his support. Lucky you having the charming Pierre to cling to. I bet he was as firm as a rock.'

'Yes, he was. Cool, calm and collected as usual.'

Something hesitant in the tone of her voice alerted Bea. She gazed curiously at her niece, drank part of her coffee, then said, 'You're not falling for Pierre by any chance, are you, dear? There's nothing between you, is there?'

For a moment Annabel hesitated. 'No, Aunt Bea, nothing at all,' she said firmly.

It gave her a sense of shock to know her words were more or less the brutal truth. There was absolutely nothing between herself and Pierre—no promise, no binding link of any kind. The love was all on her side. She had a sudden lost feeling of being adrift with no real reason for living. She longed to confide in her aunt, but it would be so pointless. It would only add to the other woman's problems, and it would not solve her own. She could not make Pierre love her any more than she could stop loving him herself.

Aunt Bea was speaking again. 'Forgive me for asking a second time, my dear, but I have to be sure.' Her smile was tender. 'While Pierre is our only hope of prising Marilyn away from her unfortunate attachment, I would hate to think you would be hurt in any way. The whole point in my having the wretched girl, apart from making sure she sleeps in her own bed at night, is to encourage her affair with Pierre.'

'I understand, Aunt Bea, and it's very sweet of you to be so concerned about me. I'll do what I can for Marilyn to help her break off her affair with the pop group!'

Bea lighted a cigarette and blew smoke away from the table. 'My poor sweet! You're a sucker like all us Staceys for feeling sorry and going all out to help others. You know,' thoughtfully, 'I don't know whether it's with writing books and studying other people material-wise, but I'm afraid I'm a wee bit sceptical regarding Marilyn. I can't help thinking we would be better employed helping someone who's in real need of help instead of a silly girl of means who has everything except common sense.'

Annabel smiled wistfully over her coffee cup. 'If you're asking my opinion, I would say she still needs someone to save her from herself, despite her fortunate position in life. Marilyn might be in love with this Kim because sticking with him calls for a lot of courage on her part. And she's only young.'

'So are you, and you don't appear to be particularly happy since she came. I thought Marilyn would be good company for you, being in your age group. Now I'm not so sure.' A worried pleat was visible between Bea's delicate brows. 'Anyway,' brightening, 'her parents will soon be back and then you and I can enjoy ourselves.'

'Dear Aunt Bea, stop worrying. I must admit I've been a little disappointed at not having you to myself. However, you have your work to do and I don't want to be under your feet all the time. Besides, I like Marilyn and I'm as anxious as you for things to work out right for her. I'm sure they will do.'

'You're a sweet child, Annabel. By the way, I'm dining out this evening with John. I want you to come along.'

'And play gooseberry?' Annabel made a wry grimace. 'Go and enjoy it. I'm sure you'll have lots of news to tell him of your trip abroad. Do I scent a romance?'

Bea tapped ash from her cigarette on to a charming china ashtray on the table. She was suddenly grave and thoughtful.

'John lost his wife two years ago in a car crash. She was driving home after opening a village fête when she crashed around a very bad bend. John was shattered. Their son, Alistair, was soon to be married and the tragedy cast a cloud over the whole village where John is the squire.'

'How terrible! Did the marriage take place?'

'Yes. But instead of the couple moving to a house of their own they moved into the ancestral home with John. They're now a complete family, very happy together. John misses his wife, which is only natural, because they were so happy together. But he leads a full life on his estate with his son. They're both the sporting type.'

'How did you meet him?'

'Jane, his wife, was an old school friend of mine. We lost touch after she married except by the usual card at Christmas and an occasional get-together in town for lunch.' Bea crushed out her cigarette. 'I'm not pretending that John isn't fond of me. I know he is. But I would never marry him. I'm too intense a person to be satisfied with second best. He gave all his love to his wife.'

'But if you love him?'

'I'm not allowing myself to go that far. I refuse to break up the unity between father and son. Besides, like me, John leads a full and busy life. So you see I don't mind in the least you dining with us this evening.'

'No, thanks, Aunt Bea. Another time, perhaps. Here's Marilyn.'

Annabel felt a sense of let-down. Nothing would have pleased her more than to see her beloved aunt settling down with some nice man. However, it was not to be. She watched her aunt gather up her morning correspondence which had arrived by the first post and after a short exchange with Marilyn the older woman went along to her study.

Marilyn's air of bravado was very apparent this morning. She was wearing an expensively cut suit in blue silk, a colour so flattering to blondes. The sun frolicked in her golden hair, but her eyes looked jaded. They flickered over Annabel's slim form in the towelling jacket and lingered on her glowing face and the silky tendrils of hair drying around her temples.

Annabel met her regard with a friendly smile. 'Do you swim, Marilyn?' she asked.

Marilyn dropped into a chair at the table as Deno appeared with fresh coffee. 'Nothing for me, Deno, only coffee,' she told him before answering Annabel. 'Yes, I do. We have a heated indoor pool at home.'

She spoke naturally. There was nothing of the boaster about Marilyn. To her everything, wealth and comfort in every form had come as naturally as breathing. Mentally, Annabel shook her head with the hope that the girl would marry someone of her own kind. She was certainly not fitted to be one of the world's Cinderellas.

She poured out the coffee and passed it across the table to her companion.

'How nice. You must miss it. Don't you miss your friends too?'

'Most of my school friends are married.' The sun glinted on the jewelled bracelet gracing her slim wrist as she picked up her cup. 'Don't you want to be married?'

Annabel had poured out another cup of coffee for herself to be companionable. 'Of course, to the right man,' she answered.

'If you ever meet him.' Marilyn drank her coffee in slow sips. 'I thought Kim was the right man for me, but now I'm not so sure. Take my advice and don't fall in love. It hurts too much. You're not yourself any more either. You become an appendage of someone else. Oh, hell, let's go out shopping.'

'All right. Don't you think you ought to eat something while I change?'

Annabel was aware that her companion was under a strain of some kind and had no wish to probe. She watched Marilyn put down her cup and take up a packet of cigarettes to light one with shaking fingers.

'I don't want anything. I've a beast of a headache.'

'Didn't you sleep very well?'

Something in her question alerted a strange gleam in the grey-green eyes. Very quietly, Marilyn said, 'You know I went out last night, don't you?'

'Yes, I do. It was accidental, though. I wasn't spying on you or anything like that. Aunt Bea wondered how you were feeling after the earth tremors and I offered to go to your room to see if you were all right.'

Marilyn studied the glowing end of her cigarette. 'Did you tell her?'

'No. I thought you wouldn't have sneaked off like you did if you'd wanted her to know.'

Marilyn bristled. 'I don't care for that sneaking off description of my leaving the house!'

Annabel looked her straight in the eyes. 'But you did sneak off, and I think you were being very unfair to Aunt Bea. As her guest you owe her some consideration. You acted as though you were ashamed of anyone knowing. Marilyn, we are your friends.'

Marilyn shrugged indifferently. 'Kim picked me up at the gate. I went to a party.' Her lips thinned. 'Why not tell Aunt Bea if you feel so strongly about it?'

'Because it's no business of mine and I know I have no right to censure you. I'm sorry. And I'm sorrier still to see you making such a mess of your life.'

Marilyn bristled. 'It's my own life to do with as I choose!'

'I agree. The only snag is the hurt you inflict upon those who care about you.'

Marilyn had the grace to look ashamed. 'I'm sorry. You're a sport, Annabel. Let's go out and forget it. And thanks for not saying anything to Aunt Bea.'

Marilyn's car ate up the miles to the city in a short time. As Bea had said, she was a competent driver and took no risks, keeping her cool in several tight corners among erratic drivers.

Annabel had put on a trouser suit of Kyoto silk. Exquisitely designed in all the pastel shades of a Japanese spring, it fitted her slender figure perfectly. Aunt Bea had sent it the previous Christmas. While it was impossible to compete with Marilyn in the way of clothes, Annabel was thankful she could, at least, dress well enough not to feel odd man out.

They parked the car and spent a pleasant morning in the more exclusive department stores where pretty dolly girls in uniform and gloves bowed them up and down escalators and thanked them for their custom.

They had lunch in an American Hotel Club where the membership was exclusively for high-ranking officers of the American forces and diplomats. Annabel was surprised to find the prices moderate.

The owner of the hotel was an old buddy of Dick Firbank, Marilyn's father. He was a retired Army major and Marilyn's godfather. He was introduced to Annabel when they entered the luxurious cocktail lounge before lunch. He was the typical soldier type, as well groomed as his waiters, sleek-haired, with piercing grey eyes and a nice smile.

After an excellent lunch during which two American officers at a nearby table tried to get acquainted, the two girls left the hotel and strolled to the park. It was cool and fresh away from the bustle and noise of the city. Gardeners clad in baggy blue cotton trousers and shirts were gathering dead winter grass and leaves together with long-handled brooms, and the greenness was dotted here and there with picnickers.

They sat down beneath a tree by a stream and Marilyn lay back to close her eyes. Annabel, to whom everything was as yet new and strangely bewildering, watched a party on a picnic nearby. It appeared to a family affair with papa-san, mama-san, married daughters and sons with their children and number one, two and three aunts and uncles. They had all removed their shoes to kneel on tatami mats which they had spread on the grass. They were orderly and quiet as they ate their lunch of sushi and cold tempura washed down with saké and beer. Mama-san sat nursing the youngest baby, a cute little fellow with a bullet head and black currant eyes which disappreared into a crease in his chubby face when he laughed.

Aware that she had been staring at them, Annabel lay down by Marilyn and looked up through the leaves of the tree. She must have fallen asleep, for she was awakened by the sound of laboured breathing. The baby belonging to the family of picnickers was bending over her face, and the effort of bending his fat little body double in order to look down at her was giving him difficulty in breathing.

When he saw her open her eyes, he chuckled and showed a perfect set of tiny teeth. Annabel was enchanted. She reached up and pulled him down against her, tickling him and loving the feel of his smooth-skinned little face against her own. Then she set him down on his feet to watch him toddle off to the family, stumbling in his baby way across the grass.

Mama-san, who had been watching them, nodded and smiled at Annabel as she reached out to take the baby back into her arms. She smiled back.

'What are you smiling at?'

Marilyn, awakened by the baby's chuckles, removed her sunglasses and sat up. After tossing a negligent glance towards the picnickers, she looked around where she was sitting.

'Did I bring my purse with me or did I leave it in the hotel?' she asked.

'I haven't seen it.'

When a search in the vicinity failed to reveal the purse, Marilyn stood up and tossed back her golden hair.

'I'd better go back to the hotel to see if it's still there. Shan't be long.'

She was gone, walking gracefully across the grass, before Annabel could offer to go with her. Poor Marilyn, she thought. The girl was far too restless to be happy. Why then did she insist upon clinging to a hopeless love? As far as she could see the girl was doomed to heartbreak with a man like Kim.

Annabel rose to her feet, adjusted her sunglasses and her shoulder bag and decided to stretch her legs. Away to her left, teenage boys were practising judo beneath the watchful eye of an elderly tutor. She paused to watch the bare feet of the boys flash through the air with the flapping of wide cream trousers against their legs as they were thrown by their teacher on to the mat—a sensible way to let off steam, she thought, while giving the boys character and confidence in their own abilities.

The tutor smiled and bowed at her as she passed, his wise old eyes appraising her youthful freshness and graceful carriage. Not wishing to be too far away when Marilyn returned, Annabel walked on to one of the picturesque bridges over the stream and gazed down into the water. The thought had occurred to her that Marilyn's discovery that her purse was missing was somehow not genuine. Had she planned it in order to go somewhere she did not want Annabel to know about? Yet why should she?

Annabel pulled up her thoughts sharply. Going back to the hotel for her purse would not take Marilyn above ten minutes. In that case she should be back any time now. Annabel lifted her head to look across the park towards the gates and her heart plummeted. Someone was striding across the grass towards her, the sun glinting on his dark hair. He walked easily with that graceful swing expressing the vitality and vigour of a naturally sound physique.

As always the sight of Pierre brought the telltale colour to her face. But she managed to calm herself before he joined her on the little bridge. Her smile was sweetly welcoming.

'Pierre, what a surprise! Have you seen Marilyn?'

'Is she not with you?'

He frowned down at her and she felt his displeasure. Or was it disappointment?

'She went to the hotel where we had lunch for her purse.'

His face deepened. 'Did she leave it behind?'

'Yes. We'd been here in the park some time before she missed it. I hope she finds it.'

'Why did you not go with her?'

'She didn't give me time to. She was off like a shot.'

He had turned his head towards the entrance to the park. The dark profile etched against the blue sky told her nothing, but his voice had an edge on it.

'Does Marilyn usually go off and leave you alone?'

'No, she doesn't. Besides, I can take care of myself.'

'Can you?' His tones softened imperceptibly and she looked up into the bantering expression he often baffled her with. 'You present tempting bait for any designing male. Do you know that?'

'No, I didn't. Thanks for the compliment. How did you know we were here in the park?'

'I happened to have lunch at the same hotel and saw you leave.'

A hand gripped her heart painfully at the thought of him lunching or having dinner there with Marilyn. He might even have gone there on the chance of meeting her.

She tried to speak lightly. 'We did some shopping this morning, then we had lunch and landed up here in the park. What a strange and wonderful country it is, so different from anywhere else.'

'Better than Paris?'

She ignored the sudden tightening in her throat. 'Not better. Very different.'

'*Ma chère*,' he said softly, looking down into her eyes, 'how very carefully you answered.'

'Did I? Everything changes. We are different too.'

'Are we, *mon enfant*?' He caught her hand, laughing down mockingly at her sudden flush. 'You are hot. Come, sit down in the shade of the trees and I will fetch a nice cool drink.'

They walked hand in hand towards the trees in sight of the party of picnickers who were now all asleep after their meal. Annabel envied their serenity and wondered if she would ever know it herself again.

Pierre peeled off his jacket and spread it on the grass for her to sit on, then he strode away to the nearest refreshment house. He was back surprisingly quickly with an iced drink for Annabel and a beer for himself. Dropping down beside her, he leaned back against the tree and took down part of his beer. Annabel did the same, to find the iced lime cool and refreshing. But she felt far from relaxed. Being with

Pierre was all the more unbearable because he was staring ahead and appeared to be totally unaware of her presence.

His sunburnt face was a bronze mask and the sun picked out reddish glints from his thick dark hair. In the tailored silk shirt, his brown throat was firm and strong, his shoulders wide and square. He looked fit and self-sufficient, and very dear. Often during the last two years she had pictured him striding alone through the crimson and gold haze of a tropical night, dining with a pretty woman in a select night club or driving along beneath brilliant neon night lights. Never had she loved him more than in that moment. Pierre was the first to break the silence.

'This man you are going to marry—is he the kind of puissant Q. C. who regards you as not being too sufficiently *ennuyée* with him to seek other man's company? *Mais vraiment*, he is taking a risk in allowing you to wander half way across the world alone.'

He had tilted an eyebrow in her direction to speak in jesting mood.

Her heart contracted. She wanted to tell him there was no other man. But his lightheartedness stung.

'You know more about being bored than I. At this very moment you could be so bored with my company that you're aching longingly for the next assignment.'

'On the contrary, I am enjoying myself too much to be *ennuyé*. I have two charming women, one American, one English, each so vastly different from the other, each so devastatingly chic and pretty.'

Annabel moistened her throat with the iced drink. 'Are we so much different? I know Marilyn is very attractive. I like her.'

'*Tiens!* Marilyn is like me, much travelled, experienced and no heart.'

'I don't agree. Marilyn has a heart. Why do you think she ...' Annabel pulled herself up short of mentioning the other girl's devotion to Kim. 'She's very loving.'

'Loving, lovely and level-headed—the latter making all the difference, *ma chère*,' he said mockingly.

'And what would you say makes me different from Marilyn?' she asked quietly, refusing to look at him.

He gazed down on the youthful curve of her chin, the glossy dark hair and the shadow of her lashes against cheeks slightly flushed.

'A moment ago you reminded me of La Belle Dame Sans Merci.' He quoted mockingly, 'Her foot was light and her eyes were wild. You were quite something when you were defending Marilyn.'

'And why shouldn't I defend my own sex? Go on. Tell me what you really think about me.'

'I like your innocence, *cher enfant*. At the moment I find it very refreshing. There are times, though, when I find it extremely irritating. You believe in love and marriage in an airy-fairy way. I've seen you sitting listening to your parents during their act. Your eyes were full of dreams. Life and love are not like that. It is not just a gentle arm around your waist and a chaste kiss or two, it is more down to earth. Men are, you know.'

This time she did meet his eyes. 'Are men all like you, seeking new thrills and ... and new women?' Something blazing in her eyes stopped him from answering. She went on blindly, wanting to hurt as he had hurt her. 'You would have me believe that, wouldn't you? Because I'm a romantic you think I'm afraid of passion, of letting myself go. What do you know about the real me? When you've never really thought of me in that light? Well, have you?'

Pierre had moved in order to see her face. His mouth twitched at her heightened colour. He leaned forward, very close. 'Have you thought of me in that light, *ma belle*?' he murmured.

Annabel made no immediate answer. She was feeling rather sick and scared of the tumult of feeling this man aroused in her. Her whole being seemed to be pulsating at his nearness. It was fantastic how his very strength could make her weak. She thought wildly, 'I hate him. I don't love him. I hate him.' But it did not help, although with each passing second she was assuming the calmness of despair.

'Go on, tease me if you enjoy it!'

She turned her head away and saw Marilyn regarding them with a smile.

Pierre returned her greeting lightly as if she had been the one woman he had been waiting to see. 'I was wondering where you had got to,' he said.

Marilyn's eyes were shining, her pink lips slightly parted. She looked to Annabel as if she had been injected with new life, as though the bad head had never been. A splash of colour stained her cheeks. Was it excitement or the pleasure of seeing Pierre? Annabel caught her breath.

He was looking at Marilyn as though he could not take his gaze away. The sunlight fell on his tanned face, sharpening the angles. The unexpected total absorption struck Annabel a mortal blow. Tears rose unbidden to her eyes and she turned her head sharply away in an effort to control them.

Through the trees, the lake was diamond-bright with brilliant patches of sunlight on the surface. A couple were rowing themselves leisurely across to one of the tiny islands in the centre. There was a blinding flash each time the oars dipped into the water. Suddenly Annabel knew. She was jealous of Marilyn, for Marilyn had a combination of toughness and allure akin to Pierre. They were two of a kind.

'Did you find your purse?' she asked Marilyn.

'Oh—er—yes, of course.' She held the missing purse aloft. 'I left it in the dining room.'

Pierre said sardonically, 'You were lucky. Sit down while I fetch you a drink.'

Annabel breathed in Marilyn's expensive perfume as she sat down to share part of Pierre's jacket beside her. Was the bright smile she flashed a little too bright? Had she really forgotten her purse? Annabel could not help but think she had looked a trifle guilty on being asked if she had found it. Annabel shook herself mentally. The pangs of jealousy were sending her sensibility haywire, she decided, and was specially nice to Marilyn, who was as effervescent as a spring morning.

'How long were you with Pierre?'

Marilyn was driving back to Aunt Bea's. The diamond bracelet on her wrist sent out dazzling flashes of light in the sun as her hands turned the car wheel expertly to thread her way through the heavy traffic.

'Not long.'

'He's fascinating, isn't he?'

Annabel, who had been watching two heavily laden cycles being propelled between the traffic with superb indifference to loss of life or limb, asked:

'Who?'

'Pierre, of course.' Marilyn put on speed and left the two cyclists behind, much to Annabel's relief. 'I don't think you're as indifferent to him as you pretend to be.'

'No? What do you want me to do—set my cap at him?'

'Goodness, no! You know, I've just discovered something. I'm beginning to grow very fond of him. Come on, admit it. Don't you think he's the most exciting man you've ever met?'

'Is that a leading question?'

'In a way. He's asked us both out this evening.'

Annabel recalled Pierre talking in a low voice to Marilyn while she herself had been engrossed in the party of picnickers nearby taking their departure. They had looked across at her and bowed their farewell and her cold heart had warmed to the gesture.

'Count me out,' she said.

'But isn't Aunt Bea dining out tonight?'

'Yes. I've promised myself an evening in with a book.'

Marilyn swung the car on to the drive of the house. 'You needn't stay at home for my sake. Pierre asked us both.'

'I'm not staying at home for your sake. I prefer an evening at home.'

She heard Pierre's car arrive that evening and the next moment Marilyn swept in, a swirling vision of pink and white draperies and silver slippers to say she was leaving. Minutes later, Annabel looked down from her window to see Pierre's head near the golden one as he opened the door of his car for Marilyn to slip inside.

Leaning unhappily against the window frame, she told herself that there must be an antidote for all the pain, part of which was self-inflicted. For Pierre had not encouraged her to fall in love with him. It had been her own fault. Had it not been for this visit to Japan, she would probably have married Francis Kerrison and found a measure of happiness with him after tucking the memory of an aggravating, loose-limbed

Frenchman away with her other souvenirs.

Later that evening, before preparing for bed, Annabel stood by her window to gaze out on to the beauty of a summer night. In a neighbouring house someone was playing a piano, a haunting melody which she was too wrapped up in unhappy thought to identify.

The music had changed into a lively dance tune when she climbed into bed. Annabel pictured Pierre dancing with Marilyn in some favourite haunt to a similar tune. Later, their bodies would merge together in the gloom as they kissed goodnight beneath her window.

At last her eyelids because as heavy as her heart. The music faded beyond her consciousness and everything became quiet.

CHAPTER FIVE

ONE thing about her visit to Japan—no one could have said with truth that it was boring. So thought Annabel when she was awakened the following morning by Marilyn clad in swimming attire sitting on her bed.

'Wake up, sleepyhead,' she said gaily. 'It's a glorious morning for a swim in the bay!'

Annabel was not long in joining her. Her troubles faded in the bright morning sun streaming through her window and she wanted to enjoy it, to forget everything that was bothering her.

'Pierre talked to me like a Dutch uncle last evening,' Marilyn confided as they strolled down to the bay arm in arm. 'He talked mainly about you.'

'About me?' Annabel was startled.

'Yes, telling me I ought to take you around and

show you the sights instead of leaving you like I did yesterday.'

Annabel knew a sharp stab of disappointment. She said frankly, 'So what I thought was a friendly gesture on your part was only brought on by something Pierre said to you.'

Marilyn was unabashed. 'Something like that. Mind you, I can see his point. You're only here for a short time and Aunt Bea has been so kind in inviting me in her home that I feel I do owe you both a little consideration.'

Something a little bitter lurked in Annabel's dark blue eyes. It was on the tip of her tongue to tell the wretched girl that Aunt Bea and herself would have been much happier if she had stayed elsewhere. However, mindful of the importance of having Marilyn there to keep an eye on her, she spoke tolerantly.

'Thanks. But I'm perfectly capable of enjoying my holiday in my own way.'

Marilyn had the grace to blush. 'I'm sorry, I shouldn't have put it so crudely. I didn't mean to sound pompous.' She gave a small laugh. 'The fact is, I resented Pierre's interest in you.'

'Now you're being silly. Why should you?'

'Because I don't want him to become too fond of you. I'm jealous.'

'You forget I've known Pierre for two years. My parents live in Paris and he knows them too. They might have asked him to keep an eye on me if they know he's come to Japan.'

'That's what worries me. You've known him for so much longer than I have. I want him to myself and not to share with anyone else.'

And whatever you want you have, thought Annabel, changing her mind about her companion. She was nothing more than a little tramp. She would not put it past her to have carried on with the rest of Kim's group, himself included. She was not the first girl to go berserk in hero-worship of a pop group. Now she wanted Pierre thrown in for good measure.

As swiftly as her anger mounted, it began to recede. Was she not forgetting that Pierre was the last hope of the Firbanks in making their daughter break off with the group? Whether Marilyn herself was worth saving was irrelevant. Besides, Pierre was too smart to be caught so easily. Suddenly, Annabel felt the need to get away by herself. They had reached the beach and she slipped out of her beach shoes.

Dropping her towelling jacket, she said heavily, 'Don't you think you ought to be off with the old love before beginning the new?'

The swim in the cool water did much to get Annabel back on to an even keel. Her smile at her companion as they dried their limbs and shrugged into their towelling jackets was genuine and friendly. Marilyn, she told herself, had been used to having her own way for so long that her personality had become subtle.

Aunt Bea had come out on to the patio where Deno had set breakfast when the two girls returned to the house. She greeted them with a 'bless you, my children' smile.

'Breakfast is ready,' she informed them. 'I hope you both have a good appetite.'

Annabel kissed her cheek before sitting down at the table. 'Did you have a nice evening, Aunt Bea?'

'Marvellous, thanks. I hope you weren't too lonely on your own. You ought to have come with us.'

'She wanted to be alone,' Marilyn chipped in, 'Pierre invited us both out and she refused to come.'

Her grey green eyes narrowed across at Annabel. 'You didn't have a man in the house, by any chance?'

'Yes. A very handsome Japanese,' Annabel replied gaily.

Bea poured out coffee, handing a cup to her niece and one to Marilyn.

'So you went out with Pierre. No need to ask if you had a good time. He's quite a heart-throb, so well groomed and essentially masculine, with the gift of making a woman feel beautiful and precious in his company. His kind are becoming rare—more's the pity, especially when you see the bewhiskered, bleary-eyed young men of today.'

Pierre. Always Pierre, Annabel thought distractedly as she swallowed her coffee much too hot. Was there no getting away from him? Better that he should declare his love for Marilyn and go away instead of staying to torment her.

Marilyn, however, had not missed Bea's carefully aimed dart at herself and her association with Kim. Her mouth curved in the slightest of insolent smiles.

'Men are much the same underneath,' she said tartly. 'I will say, though, that I recommend a Frenchman as an escort any time. They certainly know how to compliment and charm.' Her eyes veiled a curious look at Annabel, who steeled herself for the sword thrust intended for her bruised heart. 'Not to mention their technique in making love!'

Neither Bea nor Annabel had to find a reply to this because Deno came with breakfast. As he returned indoors the phone rang. Deno answering it reappeared on the patio to say Marilyn was wanted. She rose to her feet and pushed back her chair scrapingly on the tiled floor and followed Deno into the house.

She was back in minutes. 'I have to go out,' she

76

said. 'See you later.'

Her smile was brief and with a flash of long legs, she went to her room swiftly to change. Annabel spread marmalade on a finger of toast she did not really want and said nothing. It seemed no time at all before they heard Marilyn's car start up and go down the drive.

Bea had raised delicately arched brows at her guest's somewhat abrupt departure. 'If Marilyn knew what was good for her she would have gone to the States with her parents,' was her caustic comment.

Annabel had to disagree. 'Not until she's got this Kim out of her system. Distance is no object where the emotions are concerned. It doesn't make you care less about a person you care for.'

'You mean distance does make the heart grow fonder?' Bea eyed her curiously. 'Do you speak from experience or sympathy?'

Annabel laughed. 'Really, Aunt Bea! Are you seeking another plot for your new book?'

Her aunt did not smile. Her look was troubled. 'Something is troubling you, my dear. I wish you'd tell me what it is. Perhaps I could help. You're a different person from the Annabel I used to know.'

'As I told you, I'm two years older.'

'So am I. Unfortunately, that doesn't answer my question and I can see you don't want to. All right, I can take a hint. Only don't forget, a trouble shared is a trouble halved, and my shoulder is as good as ever it was to cry on.'

Annabel bit her lip, torn between telling her aunt about her insane passion for Pierre and keeping her own counsel. The latter would be the kindest course. Her aunt would only worry over a further complication of the matter in hand, namely Pierre and Marilyn getting together.

'I'm sorry, Aunt Bea.' Her smile was wistful. 'Maybe I'm allowing Marilyn's affairs to affect me too much. I certainly don't envy the mess she appears to be making of her life. Come to think about it, I don't think she thanks us for interfering.'

Bea picked up a packet of cigarettes and offered one. They both smoked for a while in silence.

'Maybe you're right, my pet.' Bea flicked a speck of tobacco from her lower lip. 'We're too softhearted.'

'Which reminds me—you must be aching to look over the notes you've made about your new book. I know you went to America to collect copy, so get cracking. I'm going out for the day.'

Her aunt tapped ash from her cigarette into an ash tray. 'You're not going on your own. I'm coming with you,' she said determinedly.

Annabel was equally determined. 'You are not in the least enthusiastic about it. I know you hate the heat and would only be pulling on your bit to get back to your typewriter. The heat doesn't bother me. Besides, I came away with the intention of not missing a thing.'

'But, my dear...'

Annabel rose to her feet. 'It isn't the slightest use. I'm going. Can I borrow the car?'

'Of course. I'll have Deno fill it up while you dress. I hope you'll be all right.' Bea crushed out her cigarette beside Annabel's in the ashtray, a worried pleat between her brows. 'Would you like Deno to go with you?'

'And leave you to answer the door to callers when you might be in the middle of an exciting plot? No, darling, Annabel is going out on her own and looking forward to it.'

78

Suddenly she was staring down at the table at the huge spider with the tortoiseshell legs that had scared her so much on the day she had run into Pierre's arms. Only she was not frightened any more. It had paused at her plate to eye a fat juicy crumb of buttered toast before looking up at her with protruding black eyes.

'Here's Mariko, your spider, Aunt Bea. I do believe he's asking my permission to eat the crumb on my plate.' She chuckled. 'Go on, take it and I'll starve,' she quipped. 'You're right, Aunt Bea, about us Staceys being suckers. We don't even stop at spiders.'

Bea grimaced at her fondly. 'I love you, Annabel. Go out and enjoy yourself—and take care. Don't be late coming home or I shall worry.'

Annabel set off in Aunt Bea's car in the opposite direction to the city of Tokyo. She drove through the little village in the bay with its shrine, station, parks and public bath houses. The heat shimmered in the hills and the tan ribbon of road twisted and turned until the wide expanse of blue sea was before her. On the rocky coast creeks formed havens for fishing boats floating picturesquely at anchor and on the slopes of the hills she saw toy wooden houses and the glimpse of an occasional pagoda roof of a temple.

At a temple resthouse overlooking the sea, she ate her package lunch prepared by Deno. Picnickers were there on their tatami mats, laughing and chattering, their tinkling happiness merging with the tinkle of bells in nearby orchards put there to scare away the birds.

It was too hot after lunch to be very energetic. Annabel parked the car in one of the tiny bays and bathed in the sea. Later she lazed in a sheltered cove with a book. On her way back she stopped at a market garden to buy flowers for her aunt, lilies and fern arranged beautifully and tied with a bow of white satin ribbon.

Aunt Bea was not in her study nor in the lounge when Annabel, after putting the car away, went indoors in search of her. But the little mouselike woman who came in daily to help Deno with the chores met her in the hall. Smiling over arms full of sweetly smelling freshly laundered linen she had brought in from the lines in the kitchen garden, she said Miss Stacey was in the kitchen. Annabel found her aunt about to pick up a tray of freshly made tea.

'Hello, my dear,' she exclaimed. 'No need to ask if you've enjoyed your day. You look positively blooming!' She beamed with pleasure and surprise at the flowers, setting down the tray. 'Lilies? For me? Aren't they lovely? Thanks.' Her fingers caressed the waxen petals. 'I'll leave them for Deno to put in water. Come along, you're just in time for a cup of tea.'

It was like old times drinking tea with Aunt Bea in the patio overlooking the garden. Annabel wanted to hold on to each pleasant relaxed moment borrowed from time, moments she had visualized while on her way to Japan. How she had looked forward to days of sightseeing and little intimate meals with her aunt. She had spared little thought for the strangeness of the country and it had never occurred to her that she would meet Pierre and be tortured anew.

Marilyn did not return for dinner that evening. Aunt Bea had ordered it at an earlier hour in order to give them plenty of time to go to see the famous Bunraku or puppet play at a theatre quite a car run out of Tokyo.

They waited until the last moment for Marilyn to arrive, but in the end they were forced to go without her.

Bea was angry. 'It's too bad of Marilyn to let us down like this. She knew I'd booked the seats for the three of us. I hate driving anywhere in a hurry, but it's no use waiting any longer.'

While Annabel sympathised with her aunt regarding Marilyn's thoughtlessness, she was not sorry they were going on their own. Marilyn's presence brought Pierre's too near, and she wanted to forget them both for one evening of quiet enjoyment.

The puppet theatre was a large brick building completely isolated from even the most remote kind of Japanese architecture. Inside, Annabel saw armchair seats set in rows closely together. To the right of the stage, which was hidden by the usual theatre curtain, was a platform for the musicians, singers and the others taking part in the production.

Aunt Bea whispered in her ear as they took their seats, 'The puppets have wooden heads with real hair and a bamboo frame for a body. Mechanism in the neck of the puppet moves all parts of the body, eyes, brows, mouth, arms and even fingers realistically. It's incredible the way they are manipulated.'

The curtain rose on a typical garden scene reminiscent of the willow pattern with gnarled trees silhouetted like black velvet against blue skies and still bluer water stapled by hump-back bridges. The narrator then came on the stage to announce the play. Dressed entirely in black, he was one of the three men who manipulated the puppets, who were all of four foot high and necessitated their presence on the stage in the background.

Immediately after the announcement a samisen, a three-stringed Japanese guitar, strummed and a deep masculine voice began to sing. The puppets were then carried on the stage by the three black-clad manipulators who stood behind the dolls, and the play began.

So cleverly were the puppets manipulated that instantly they became deliciously human and very much alive. They breathed, walked, knelt, bowed, sat or lay down and turned their eyes and heads with their eyebrows and mouths moving realistically.

Lights, cleverly placed, changed their expressions as they went through the whole gamut of emotions; grief, rage, sorrow, laughter and expressions of hauteur. The costumes, like the scenery, were fabulous and there were many changes of costume achieved simply by transferring the head of the puppet from one costumed frame to another.

Musicians, singers, voices and manipulators worked together in a high standard of interpretation, adding pathos and sincerity to the action. Annabel loved every minute of it and left the theatre starry-eyed and enriched by the experience.

Marilyn was the last to come down to breakfast the next morning. She came into the dining room jauntily in an exquisite silk trouser suit in black covered with hand-painted flowers and birds. Her sandals were open-toed showing red-lacquered nails and her golden hair had a brittleness about it which was reflected in her grey-green eyes.

Her apology to Bea for not returning the previous evening for the visit to the puppet theatre was casual. She had gone to see a sick friend and had not noticed the time.

Aunt Bea said coolly, 'You might have rung up to say you wouldn't be back in time.'

'I did,' was the unabashed reply, 'but Deno said you'd already left for the theatre.'

Deno appeared in that moment with the morning mail, several letters and packages for Bea and a letter for Marilyn which she hastily pushed into the pocket of her suit. She had favoured Annabel with a half smile and looked unrepentant. Annabel thought she looked keyed up and restless, and noticed that she ignored the jam waffles Deno had prepared specially for her. As usual, she smoked a lot and drank several cups of coffee.

The visit to the theatre had given Annabel a sense of wellbeing. Marilyn's problems did not affect her this morning, neither did she think of Pierre. The weather was again warm, the sun shone and she could hear the little Japanese daily singing as she hung out washing in the kitchen garden.

'Do eat your waffles, Marilyn,' she said lightly. 'Deno will think they're not to your liking if you leave them. I'll join you in one, if I may?'

Marilyn said petulantly, 'Have them all. I don't feel hungry.' But she did eat them when she saw Annabel enjoying hers.

Aunt Bea did not linger at the table. Saying something about an important letter she had opened which needed answering straight away, she left the two girls and went to her study.

Annabel swallowed the last appetising morsel of waffle and wiped her fingers on her serviette. Her smile across the table was warm and frindly.

'I'd like a sauna bath, face pack, hair shampoo, pedicure, manicure, in fact the whole beauty treatment which I believe they do so well here in Japan,' she said conversationally. 'Can you recommend anywhere?'

'Sure. A simply marvellous place not far from the Ginza. You'll feel wonderful after the massage. They're so good at it.' Marilyn brightened. 'I'll take you if you like and we can meet for lunch at the

American Club hotel, say between one and two o'clock.'

The beauty salon was all Marilyn had said. The skilled hands Annabel passed through, while being light and swift, were dedicated and painstakingly applied. It was midday when she finally emerged with a sense of wellbeing, her dark hair perfumed and shining, her whole being all aglow and deliciously fresh.

Marilyn had not arrived at the hotel when she strolled through the rooms where the visitors and guests were assembled. The desk clerk said Miss Firbank had not been in but he would let her know the moment she arrived.

She ordered a coffee in the lounge, deciding against going in to lunch until Marilyn arrived.

The place was swarming with visitors, mostly men, who seemed to be attending a conference. One or two of them cast a look of appraisal her way which she was too busy watching the door to notice. Gradually everyone seated around her drifted into the dining room until she was the only one left sitting in the lounge.

Presently a pageboy looked in, eyed her contemplatively for several seconds, then made his way across the thick carpet towards her.

He bowed. 'Miss Stacey?' he asked, proud of his English. Annabel nodded. 'Miss Firbank say will Miss Stacey meet her at the Cherry Tree Club on Forty-ninth Street for lunch.'

Before she could ask him to call her a taxi, he was summoned away and Annabel was left to make her way out of the hotel into the bright sunshine. Adjusting her sunglasses, she was looking round for a taxi when someone caught her arm.

Pierre said, 'Annabel! Are you alone?'

Relief came in a thankful gasp. She looked up at him. 'Pierre! How glad I am to see you. I'm supposed to be meeting Marilyn at the Cherry Tree Club for lunch and I was hoping the taxi driver would understand me.'

He looked at his watch. 'I know the Cherry Tree Club. You're a little late for lunch. At least, you will be by the time you get there through the dense traffic. I have a table already booked at this hotel, so you had better dine with me,' he said firmly.

'But I've just come out of there. Marilyn was meeting me there for lunch and then changed her mind for some reason. Shall I be in the way ... I mean ... are you dining alone?'

He smiled down at her and her heart jerked. *'Mais pourquoi pas, mignonne?* Do not worry. As it happens the friend I was dining with has been delayed, so there is no problem.'

He took her elbow and they walked back into the hotel. A waiter met them at the entrance to the dining room to conduct them to a reserved table. Diners looked at them as they walked between them, the pretty sparkling girl and the virile, very attractive man. Annabel, pleased she was looking her best, smiled at him across the table as he sat down opposite to her.

'Eh bien,' he drawled. 'You look good enough to eat.'

Pleasure and pain mingled inside her. 'Don't tell me you're that hungry!' He passed her the menu and she shook her head. 'You choose.'

He did so and while they waited for service he asked what she had been doing since they last met.

Annabel told him about the puppet show and how

85

she had enjoyed it. He watched her as he listened, his dark eyes on the sheen of her glossy dark hair, her deep blue eyes eloquent and warm, her pink parted lips and pretty hands which she used so expressively when she talked.

Once his hands had covered hers and he had told her banteringly that it was an effective way of keeping her quiet. How she had laughed! She was more subdued than the Annabel he remembered, and he wondered why. When she paused, rather breathless, at the end of her praise of the puppets, she dropped her hands into her lap, aware of his eyes on them.

The next moment she was smiling. 'Now it's your turn to tell me about the hair-raising experiences you've encountered. I'm not surprised at your reluctance to settle down.'

'*Au contraire*,' he answered lightly, lazily, 'while there is much to be said about riding on the crest of a wave, the ordinary calmer waters look devilishly tempting at times.'

Her blue eyes meeting his were wide and steady. 'Even so, I'm sure you can shrug off that feeling easy enough. Unless,' here her heart faltered, 'unless some woman sailing on those calmer waters has made them more inviting.'

She hardly seemed to breathe as she watched his dark features and despaired of the formidable obstacles dividing them. She waited with bated breath, waited for him to ... But the ensuing silence was unbearable. The words were out before she could prevent them. 'Well? Is it a woman?'

His strange half smile in which cynicism and some other half-suppressed emotion lingered became more pronounced. '*Peut-être*,' he said laconically.

So he had not denied it. His veiled 'Perhaps', meant

only one thing. There was a woman—Marilyn. Annabel sat very straight and still facing him in the manner of a person who had been mortally wounded by some hidden foe but who was valiantly hiding the fact. Her first astounding thought was that she felt nothing only a numbness intruding in all her joints.

Pierre was looking at her with an expression she could not understand—searching, quizzical—she could not say. But there was a hint of bitter humour, and she wondered why.

The waiter appeared with their aperitifs. Pierre picked his up. Mockingly he gave her the toast. 'To your Q. C., *ma chère reine*. May your quiet waters lift you on to the crest of a wave.'

'Now you're laughing at me! Francis is not the staid Englishman you imagine him to be. He knows how to bring effervescence to the quietest water, I assure you.'

She drank in response to his toast, surprised that she could still swallow in spite of an aching restriction in her throat.

The woman paused at their table like a grey apparition. 'Why, Annabel! This is a surprise. Francis didn't mention that you were coming abroad.'

Annabel stiffened inwardly and looked up rather blankly at the tall, thin, aristocratic woman, impeccably dressed, who was regarding her with no particular warmth in her expression. Mrs Kerrison had the repressive manner that demanded respect and a kind of awe. Usually it affected her friends with a nervous desire to placate her. On the other hand, Annabel knew it had an opposite effect on herself.

In her unbiased opinion, Mrs Kerrison was a snob of the first water and a forceful personality where her husband and son were concerned. Francis had inherited her stern aquiline features and obstinate chin which were more acceptable in a man than a woman.

Annabel was used to the woman's analytical regard of herself and was well aware of the resentment she harboured against someone who threatened to steal her son. Few mothers of sons who had remained single as long as Francis took kindly to being replaced in his affections by a wife. They had possessed their sons too long to relish relinquishing them.

She replied conventionally to the older woman's greeting and calmly introduced Pierre.

'*Enchanté, madame.*'

Pierre was on his feet with a bow and Mrs Kerrison responded instantly to his charm. His immaculate appearance and ineffaceable quality of race pleased her fastidiousness. She was as susceptible as anyone to a charming man.

She unbent a little to smile down on Annabel. 'Are you here on holiday or paying a visit to the Trade Fair?'

'I'm visiting an aunt,' Annabel replied.

'Indeed?' The arched eyebrows lifted and the shrewd grey eyes slid over Annabel's youthful freshness. For the second time that day Annabel was glad of her visit to the beauty salon. 'I had no idea you had relatives in this part of the world.'

Annabel would have loved to be able to produce a Japanese aunt or two if only to see Mrs Kerrison's face. She smiled impishly at the thought.

'My aunt settled here two years ago. She's a writer.'

'Perhaps you would join us for lunch,' Pierre broke in smoothly.

'We've already dined. My husband has been called to the phone and I was on my way out to join him when I saw Annabel. I'm afraid I shan't see you again,

Annabel. We leave this evening for London. I'll tell Francis I've seen you.' Her manner struck Annabel like a veiled threat.

Like anything you will, she thought, especially about me being with a man. She watched the grey-clad figure walk erectly and proudly out of the dining room, realizing that she had completely forgotten about Francis Kerrison until Pierre's mention of him. He had completely disappeared from her life. Now it seemed that fate was deliberately pushing them together again, that even in his absence Francis was offering her the chance to escape from the despair and the pain of unrequited love.

After lunch, Pierre insisted upon driving her to the Cherry Tree Club. In the centre of the town the traffic was congested and the journey was a slow crawl. The brilliant afternoon sun sprayed a garish light over banners, signs and lanterns hanging over the shops and Pierre presently parked the car by a warehouse for them to continue on foot through the narrow streets.

Walking beside him in the bustling thoroughfare, Annabel breathed in the strange aromatic scents of over-population and the music blaring from transistor sets and shop doorways struck harshly on her ears.

Pierre had taken her elbow in his strong fingers and led her around a corner into a street of neat little brown houses with latticed windows and gay lanterns. The tinkling music of a samisen and laughter came from one of them as the door opened and two pretty geisha girls came out. The bright kimonos of a rich silk brocade contrasted oddly with the deadpan white-ness of their little painted faces as they drifted by, tiny, slender and doll-like with the soft movement of a scented breeze.

As they passed, the silver ornaments in their elaborately coiffured hair tinkled gaily and Annabel smiled at them, entranced.

'How lovely they are,' she exclaimed. 'Like delicious little dolls.'

Pierre looked down at her mockingly. 'They're probably thinking the same about you and envying your lovely complexion.'

The little street of neat wooden houses led off into a small square. It was closed to traffic and there were seats set beneath cherry trees where old men sat asleep with their dogs at their feet.

The Cherry Tree Club had its entrance between two cherry trees. It stood between a cinema and a public bath house.

'It looks deserted,' Pierre said, eyeing the closed doors. 'Yet they must be expecting you.' His keen eyes moved to the opening between the club and the cinema. 'We are evidently expected to go around to the back entrance.'

They walked down the passageway to a courtyard and a door which Pierre opened. As he did so the sound of a piano being played lazily came from the direction of thickly carpeted stairs to their left. After the bright sunlight the interior looked dim and Annabel stumbled at the first step. Pierre gripped her arm and they climbed the stairs into a deeply carpeted foyer with several sliding doors.

Pierre opened the first one which led into a dimly lit room with heavy velvet drapes and they trod on the same thick carpet from the stairs. It was a large room with dining tables set around a wide expanse of polished wooden floor. The soft gleam of silver and flower arrangements on the white tablecloths drew the eyes to a dais at the far side of the room.

It was occupied by a group of four musicians, two

with guitars, one with a sheet of music and the fourth idly strumming the piano. They were carelessly dressed in tee-shirts and jeans and wore their hair in a depressing length which added an air of general untidiness emphasised by the straggling beards and sideboards. Marilyn was there, her golden hair incongruous against the unkempt hair of the young man holding the music as they bent over it. She swung round as Pierre and Annabel entered the room and there was a seemingly endless silence as they looked at each other across the unoccupied sea of tables.

In dismay, Annabel saw that she had brought Pierre unwittingly to the club where Kim and his group were appearing. Marilyn was the first to recover herself. She came forward gracefully, her eyes hard, her smile wary.

'Annabel!' she cried. 'Wherever have you been? I waited lunch for you a long time before giving you up.' Her little laugh held no mirth. 'Don't tell me that you got lost and had to appeal to Pierre to bring you.'

A strange feeling of crisis sucked Annabel's throat dry. She spoke firmly and without anger.

'I didn't get your message until the pageboy with whom you had left it contacted me. Had you left it with the clerk at the reception counter I would have received it much sooner instead of sitting wondering what had happened to you. By then it was too late to come here for lunch, so I dined with Pierre.'

Marilyn laughed, in no way perturbed. Her voice was honey-sweet for Pierre's benefit.

'Sorry, but Kim asked me to come to lunch here. The girl singer who has been appearing with them is ill and they've asked me to take her place.'

Pierre shot a sardonic glance at the group on the dais.

'I hardly think your parents will approve,' he said mildly.

Marilyn was vividly amused. 'It's only temporary. Come and meet the group. They were quite famous in the States.'

She took Pierre's arm possessively and drew him towards the stage, leaving Annabel to follow. She did not do so immediately, for she knew Marilyn was annoyed with her for bringing Pierre. The stale atmosphere, a mixture of food and cigarettes filled her with a longing for the sweet clean air outdoors.

Suddenly she was aware of the pianist coming towards her.

'Well, well,' he exclaimed boldly. 'And where has Marilyn been hiding you? I'm Don Cook. Delighted to meet you, Annabel.'

He held out his hand smiling broadly. He was dark-skinned with heavy eyebrows over the bold dark eyes, a ladykiller if ever there was one. Putting out her hand, Annabel wondered why his face was familiar, and remembered seeing him with Marilyn on the day she passed them in Aunt Bea's car. She drew her hand away when he would have held it longer, feeling no more impressed by him than she had been then. Politely returning his greeting, she moved up with him to the rest of the group where Marilyn introduced her to Kim.

He was slightly built and his fair hair rioted in tiny curls. His beard, she decided, covered a weak chin. He spoke with a Harvard accent and his smile was white, but he looked drawn and ill.

The other two young men, Ken and Wally Knox, were twins. Brown-haired and freckled, they were very much alike.

'What about a date?'

Don whispered in her ear under cover of the general conversation. Of the group, Annabel found him the least likeable. The others were not too bad if, as her aunt had remarked, one had time to probe beneath the face fungus. But they all looked uncouth in comparison with the immaculate and conventionally dressed Pierre.

Annabel felt her love for him bring a lump to her throat. He was looking at Marilyn with much the same intentness as he had used on previous occasions. She looked very young, very attractive in the pretty trouser suit when, taking the copy of music in her hand, she motioned to Don to come to the piano.

Apart from a certain husky appeal, her voice was not outstanding. But she had been well tutored in the art of putting the cute little number she sang across to the audience. It was obvious that Kim was the brains and the gifted one behind the group, for it was he who watched her every move.

'What is your opinion, *mon enfant*?'

Pierre had taken Annabel to a chair at the nearest table and, after handing around cigarettes, was smoking one himself. Annabel, who was the only one not smoking, looked away from his mocking eyes and mouth and saw Marilyn conferring with Kim over a second sheet of music.

'Very good for a beginner,' he said without rancour. 'Fortunately, the song was a good one. With the right songs, I would say she'll get by.'

There was tolerant humour in his voice. He leaned back against the wall behind her, much too near for her peace of mind.

'She has what it takes to get by—a bright disposition, a degree of independence and a certain amount of sex appeal.'

'Is that how you like your women?' she asked daringly.

He cocked a tantalizing brow. 'I like women to be feminine and honest. Frenchwomen particularly.'

'Naturally, since you are a Frenchman. Would you agree to your wife carrying on with her career after you were married?'

'You mean, if I were to marry? One career is enough for marriage.' He leaned forward dangerously near to tap ash from his cigarette on to an ashtray on the table where she sat. 'With me it would be all or nothing.' Then, after a brief pause, he added with apparent irrelevence, 'Do you want a career if you marry your Q. C?'

'Goodness, no! I want children and a home.'

'Then you have the right man in your Francis. Not a world-weary journalist who, at times, would give you hell tearing up roots and heading for heavens knows where.' He stubbed out his cigarette with unnecessary force and looked at his wrist watch. '*Pardon*, I have to leave for an appointment. Do not forget our date for tonight. I shall call far you at seven-thirty. *Au revoir*.'

Somewhat dazedly, she watched him take his leave of Marilyn and the group before striding from the room. She had forgotten that today was Thursday and that he had made a date with her. What could she do? Something had upset him, and she could only guess it was seeing Marilyn talking so intimately with Kim. If he had been ignorant as to their association before he was quick-witted enough to grasp the situation as it stood.

Annabel quivered. Was he deliberately insisting upon her keeping their date to show Marilyn that two could play at the game she was playing? The trouble was, there was no avoiding it. To plead illness would only alarm her aunt and arouse her suspicions regarding Pierre and herself.

Miserably, she was aware that Marilyn was about to sing again. Her second song came nowhere near the appeal of the first. Was the lack of sparkle due to the fact that Pierre was no longer there? Or was it the song?

When Annabel left the Cherry Tree Club at four o'clock, it was in a taxi alone. Marilyn was staying behind to practise for another hour or so. It was evident that Kim sought for perfection and he hoped to reach somewhere near it in presenting his new temporary singer.

CHAPTER SIX

ANNABEL was in her room dressing for her date with Pierre that evening when the phone rang. Her aunt had left earlier to attend a literary dinner.

It was Marilyn. 'Hello, Annabel. Thank goodness you're in. Will you be a pet and bring my gold brocade evening gown to the club? You know—the one with the matching nylon stole. It'll be just the thing to wear tonight for my act. I'd come to fetch it myself, only I'm fagged out. We've been rehearsing until now and I must rest before the show.'

Annabel drew a deep breath. 'But, Marilyn, I can't! I'm expecting Pierre at any moment. We're dining out.'

'What about Deno? He'll bring it.'

'Deno is out, and Aunt Bea has gone to a dinner.'

Her hand tightened on the receiver. An excuse to get out of dining with Pierre? But it had come too late

—much too late, for there was a peremptory knock on her door and she bade whoever it was come in.

Pierre strolled in nonchalantly, tanned, fit and virile in evening dress. Annabel had the sensation of being overpowered. His domination of her was as strong as the man itself. She was frightened and angry to find herself yielding rapidly to his charm and the getting of his own way.

'I found no one about, so I came right up. You do not mind?' He cocked a curious eye at the phone in her hand.

'No,' she answered, covering up the mouthpiece. 'Marilyn is on the phone. Perhaps you'd care to speak to her. She's at the Cherry Tree Club.'

'But certainly.'

Annabel was very conscious of herself and painfully conscious of him as he closed the door and came straight across the room to where she stood.

'Hello, Marilyn, this is Pierre. How is the practising going?' The brown fingers brushing her own as he took the receiver sent a tingling sensation through Annabel's body and she moved away to gaze out of the window. 'Yes ... yes,' he was saying. 'You have? *Pauvre enfant!*' There was a tender smile in his voice. 'Yes, we will come along. With two such alarming critics you cannot do other than give a fine performance. *A bientôt.*'

Annabel heard the click of the receiver and seconds later felt him behind her.

'So,' he said softly in her ear, 'we dine at the Cherry Tree Club.'

'If you say so,' she said in a toneless voice.

During his conversation with Marilyn on the phone, she had wished desperately that she could have flown off out of her window like Peter Pan. It worried

96

her to realise how she had changed and was still changing. She was becoming like a jelly fish. First she had not wanted to dine with him, had actually been scared of being alone with him. Now she wanted it more than anything else in the world.

'What is this, *ma chère*? You do not wish to go?' His hands were on her slim shoulders turning her round to face him. 'We will not go, of course, if you do not want to.'

The gentle teasing tone he had used with Marilyn was no more. The note implied a demand rather than a question. He evidently knew what love was. Marilyn could make him aware of it, but not Annabel Stacey. You're a fool, she thought. He's never loved you. Why not accept it?

'You ... don't mind altering your plans?' she asked at last tentatively. 'It's such short notice. I don't mind where we go.'

She nearly added, 'As long as I'm with you,' and bit it back with an effort. While speaking, she had successfully avoided meeting his eyes until the long silence which followed forced her to do so. What she surprised in his face brought a rush of words to her lips and the final blow to her hope that they ever become close.

'I'll go to fetch the dress and stole.'

His hands dropped and she left the room blinded by tears. For beneath the enigmatic look in his dark eyes there had been something she knew only Marilyn could put there. She was still fumbling for the *mot juste* when she reached Marilyn's room.

As she sat beside Pierre with the dress carefully folded on the back of the seat between them it seemed to Annabel that Marilyn herself was actually sitting there. Her perfume filled the car. Perhaps Pierre was conscious of it too, for he said, 'I had planned on taking you to a place run by a journalist friend of mine in the hills outside Tokyo. However, we can go another time.'

'Sounds delightful,' she answered, knowing that there would not be another time.

The road was widening now on the outskirts of the city where traffic was slowed down by the tempo of city night life. Pierre swung on to side roads less congested with traffic and put on speed.

'How long has Marilyn been associating with this pop group?'

The unexpected question alerted Annabel and put her on her guard. So he had known nothing about it! In that moment she almost hated Marilyn for what she was doing to them all.

'I've no idea,' she said.

'I ask because this Kim seems to be her cavalier of the moment.'

'Naturally. She's thrilled and excited at the prospect of actually being a star, if only for a night.'

Pierre digested this in silence. After a pause during which he turned the car adroitly round one or two tricky bends, he said, 'Did you notice anything unusual about him?'

Annabel thought hard recalling the rather drawn young face and jaded eyes. Then she was sitting up straight on a note of surprise.

'Why, yes. His right arm was bent all the time. He never straightened it. It was almost as if he had it in a sling.'

'Exactly.'

She looked at his set profile curiously. 'Does it mean anything particularly? He could have injured it in an accident—or it could be arthritis.'

'I wish it were something of that kind. It is permanently bent because he has been injected too often with drugs. The arm is irrevocably damaged.'

Annabel spoke in a hushed whisper. 'Are you sure?'

'He is a drug addict all right and on the way out. I've seen too many of them not to mistake the signs.'

'You mean there's no chance for him? That he's still taking them now?'

Pierre slowed down and parked the car by the warehouse as he had done on their last visit to the club. Then he turned to look down at her with his arm resting on the car wheel. In the brief pulsating silence that followed Annabel's hands tightened in her lap. His nearness moved her profoundly.

'I am sure of it,' he said at last. His voice sharpened as he glanced at the dress on the back of the seat between them. 'What I am not sure about is that Marilyn is not in it too.'

Annabel felt a cold shiver ripple over her body. 'I don't think she could be. Marilyn is far too level-headed. Besides . . .' She stopped.

He looked at her in a way she did not understand and she wondered what was passing through his mind. All the bitterness and disappointment he had brought into her life, all her love for him was forgotten. She did not think of herself at all; only of Marilyn and her utter foolishness.

'Go on,' he commanded. 'Finish what you were saying.'

She was trembling a little. Head bent, she whispered, 'I don't believe any man would deliberately destroy the woman he loves. Hurt, perhaps, but not destroy.'

'So Marilyn and Kim are in love with each other?'

'I didn't say that. I don't think Marilyn is in love

with Kim. I think it began with a kind of hero-worship and ended with pity for him.'

Pierre sat silent, looking out through the windscreen of the car at nothing in particular. Then he opened the door of the car and came round to help her out.

They covered the short distance to the Cherry Tree Club in silence, to be met at the door by a little woman in a kimono who relieved Annabel of the dress and stole. Following them up the stairs, she left them, presumably to take the dress to Marilyn, and they entered the dining room.

A table had been reserved for them in a secluded corner with a good view of the centre of the floor. Annabel sat down, noticing that the other tables were rapidly filling up with a cosmopolitan crowd. Two young Japanese couples sat at the next table out to enjoy an evening western style. Annabel found intense pleasure in watching them, much to Pierre's amusement.

'How beautifully they behave,' she said, seeing the delight on their faces as each course of the meal was laid before them. 'Everything they do and say is accompanied by modest courtesy and gracefulness. They're so full of life and good spirits that they make one feel jaded.'.

His laughing regard was openly mocking. 'Shall I tell you what they are thinking about us?' The dark eyes teased. 'They are thinking what a charming couple, the girl so tenderly sweet and *jolie* with a tantalizing touch of English reserve. The man, so happy to spend the rest of his life with the little English flower who will give him many sons. See, it is all there on their deadpan little faces.'

Annabel looked at the pretty doll-like women with

their beautiful jet black hair and lovely slanting eyes. Returning their smile, she writhed inwardly. Please, Pierre, her heart begged, stop torturing me!

To her relief the lights suddenly lowered. Kim and his group were on the stage. A guitar plucked at the silence twanging softly, so softly that it vibrated on the air of the room. Gradually the group took up the melody and the room was filled with soft sweet music. The number was cleverly put over, a tempting little titbit for whetting the appetite of an appreciative audience.

Two more numbers followed, each one ingeniously presented, then Marilyn. As the last notes quivered into silence a silvery torch-like beam slanted down on to the centre of the polished floor. Annabel stared at it fascinated as Marilyn appeared as though fashioned from the golden shaft of light, a golden girl in the sheath evening dress and nylon stole draped around her shoulders.

For several seconds she seemed to be at a loss. Then the fugitive expression of fear, the pause of irresolution, were dismissed by a dainty little gesture, a kind of little-girl bow before she began to sing.

The musical background was a soft accompaniment of sweet sounds. The lights changed to rainbow hues, catching the sequin threads of the nylon stole when Marilyn flung her arms out wide on the last notes of a pulsating song. She certainly gave it all she had, and the audience loved it.

She sang several more songs. Then it was over and she was joining Annabel and Pierre at their table.

'Well? How was I?' she asked as Pierre pulled out a chair for her.

'*Magnifique*!'

He laughed down at her. He ordered champagne

and they drank to her success. Marilyn, two vivid spots of colour on her cheeks, ate very little but drank thirstily of the champagne. The group were playing dance music and diners got up to dance between courses. Kim was strumming a guitar. He had probably been the pianist before his arm became stiff, Annabel mused unhappily, shaken by the appalling tragedy of him being hooked on drugs.

She knew she ought to feel exultant, because Marilyn's success that evening could mean she would never break now with the group. She could even become their star singer—and that would put Pierre out of the running. Yet Annabel felt far from happy. She was afraid for Marilyn, whose success that evening seemed to have sealed her fate.

Her first impression had been that the American girl was strong-willed and level-headed and knew what she wanted. Looking at her now, her eyes sparkling with champagne and gradually becoming inebriated, she wondered.

She watched Marilyn jump to her feet as the group began to play a snappy dance tune.

'Dance with me, Pierre!' she cried.

He laughed and allowed her to pull him to his feet. 'If you desire it, *ma chère*. On one condition—that you have no more to drink.'

'Go right ahead,' Annabel said lightly on meeting his dark eyes. 'It's Marilyn's night. No other night will ever be quite the same as this for her.'

Wistfully, she saw Pierre take Marilyn in his arms and glide over the floor, saw the lovely lines of her figure melt against him as he swung her out of the path of another couple. The Japanese diners at the next table were also dancing, the kimonos of the two women exquisite in the changing lights. Then Pierre and Marilyn passed by. They were looking into each other's eyes and smiling as though enjoying a private joke.

Aunt Bea was waiting up for them when Pierre drove the two girls home. She heard of Marilyn's successful evening from the girl herself, who insisted at the end of a rather gabbled version that champagne was called for to celebrate the occasion.

Bea observed shrewdly, 'You look as though you'd already taken your share. One drink, then it's bed for both of you.'

Marilyn pouted. She had insisted upon Pierre coming into the house for a drink and had hung on to him possessively. Annabel felt in need of her bed and did not demur when, after the toast which Pierre poured, her aunt sent her to bed.

Marilyn went to see Pierre off, saying the night air would do her good. On entering her room, Annabel was drawn to her window by the sound of their voices down below. Pierre was standing with Marilyn by his car in the driveway. She was looking up at him and moving closer. The soft murmur of their voices ceased as his arms went round her and he bent his head.

Annabel could bear no more. Like a sleepwalker, she turned and began to undress.

It was eight o'clock when Annabel awoke. To her surprise she had slept soundly and was quite ready to meet the new day. The house was quiet when she put on her swim-suit and towelling jacket for a swim in the bay.

In the hall, she met Deno bringing in the milk and the morning papers. He smiled approvingly at her swimming attire saying it was a lovely day. She liked Deno and regretted not being able to get to know him more in the short time she was to be there.

With her mind and spirit bruised, she turned to the beauty of her surroundings. Tucking her towel more securely under her arm, she thrust her hands into the pockets of her towelling jacket and walked thoughtfully down to the beach.

Since seeing Marilyn in Pierre's arms last evening things seemed to have resolved themselves. She need no longer hold herself subjective to the bondage which loving Pierre had meant. The fact that he cared for Marilyn had not changed what she herself felt for him. That insuperable thing would always be there, and she could view it now with a certain degree of resignation.

After her swim, feeling considerably refreshed, Annabel returned to the house to breakfast alone. Aunt Bea appeared as she was pouring her second cup of coffee.

'Annabel! How nice to see you,' she smiled as she sat down and accepted a cup of coffee. 'You're up early after a late night. How young and fresh you look! Your face is glowing and you have a peach of a tan.' She sighed. 'What it is to be young and resilient and to wake up after only half a night's sleep as fresh as a newly plucked lettuce.' Her smile was tender. 'You've blossomed into a beautiful young woman, my pet. And yet ...' She cocked her head on one side and regarded her niece thoughtfully, 'although I kind of go for that eloquent sadness in those deep blue eyes, I much prefer the old laughing, mischievous Annabel.'

'If I wear half as well as you, Aunt Bea, I shall be satisfied. I think being away from the pressures and anxieties of everyday life contributes so much to one's well being.' Her clear blue eyes took in her aunt's still youthfully slim figure and relaxed air. 'Being happy and contented hasn't added to your weight. It's amazing how you keep so slim.'

Bea spread marmalade liberally on her toast. 'Being a writer might account for that. While I'm working on a book I don't eat between meals, I'm much too busy.'

'I hope my coming here hasn't delayed you in that respect. I enjoy going around on my own, as I've told you before.'

'It's wonderful to have you, my dear. You have no idea how I've looked forward to it. I'm only sorry we have to have to have Marilyn here at this time. What about staying on longer than the month you've planned? The Firbanks won't be staying long in the States. I could take you round then to all my friends and we could really let our hair down.'

Annabel bit her lip. To stay on, to see Pierre and Marilyn announce their engagement and be expected to share in their happiness, was more than her kind of courage could take. Yet the thought of never seeing Pierre again was shattering.

She said lightly, 'Do stop worrying. There'll be other holidays. Now tell me, how is the book going?'

'Fine.' Bea turned to smile at Deno, who appeared with fresh coffee. 'Thanks, Deno. Another cup, Annabel? Do have one with me.' Then, when her niece obediently passed her cup to be refilled, 'Was Marilyn so good last evening?'

'Yes. It was amazing how she captivated the audience. They loved her.'

'Quite an unexpected turn of events,' dryly. 'I'm wondering how her parents will take it. Not very well, I'm afraid.'

Annabel accepted her coffee politely, staring down at the delicate gold tracing around the edge of the cup, seeing again Marilyn's golden head thrown back in triumph at the end of her act.

'I see what you mean. While she's only doing the act temporarily you're thinking it could be a permanent engagement which would make her one of the group?'

She kept silent on the fact of Kim taking drugs. There was nothing to be gained by telling her aunt, who would feel it her duty to pass the news on to the Firbanks. Apart from adding to their anxieties where their daughter was concerned, there was nothing to be gained by it.

'I did at first. But when Marilyn came in last night looking kissed and dreamy-eyed after seeing Pierre off, I didn't feel so disturbed about it. What do you think?'

Annabel quivered. Scarcely knowing what she was doing, she put down her coffee and picked it up again. Her hands were shaking and she felt suddenly cold and clammy. She spoke without raising her eyes, painfully aware of her aunt's shrewd look.

'Upon reflection I would say it's possible that her success last evening could contribute to her final break with Kim. I'm of the opinion that she's fostered a kind of hero-worship for the group. And now she's actually become one of them this feeling could frizzle out.'

Bea nodded. 'I hope you're right. I can't see Pierre allowing her to carry on with a career, especially with the group if they do make a match of it. He's far too much male to be anyone's lapdog. Frankly, I shall be relieved when she does reach some kind of a decision.'

'Don't worry about it. Things have a way of working themselves out.' Annabel smiled at her aunt, apparently unmoved. 'Marilyn will change if she marries Pierre—he'll see to that.'

Annabel finished her coffee and sat back in her chair with no great emotion, not even a feeling of bitterness. She had told herself many times what a fool she was to love someone who was hardly aware that she existed. Besides, had she not read somewhere that true love was usually recognised on both sides and was never one-sided? Had Pierre and herself been meant for each other he would have fallen in love with her as she had with him.

'Any plans for today?'

Aunt Bea's voice roused Annabel from unhappy thoughts. She pulled herself together. 'Nothing in particular. Why?'

'Some friends of mine are coming this evening. There's a fiesta on in the town and we usually do the rounds just for fun. Like to go?'

'Very much.'

They had finished their breakfast when Deno brought the post. Bea had an important big manilla envelope which she took to her study and Annabel had one letter from Francis Kerrison. In it he said how much he missed her and was waiting for her return. Annabel wondered what he would think when his mother returned home to tell him she had seen her with Pierre. Not that it mattered. She knew now that she could never marry Francis.

Towards lunchtime a sudden breeze came up and the sky darkened for rain. Deno set the midday meal in the dining room and Annabel went down to find Marilyn already there.

'Hello,' she said brightly, sitting down and picking up her table napkin. 'How does it feel to be a star overnight?'

Marilyn looked up from the generous slice of melon on her plate. 'I never realised it was so easy. I still can't believe it.'

'It isn't. You were very good. How do you feel about Kim now you've joined the bandwagon?'

'I don't know. All I remember of last evening was seeing Pierre off when we came back to the house.'

Annabel swallowed a portion of juicy melon with an effort. 'What happened? Did ... he propose?'

'No. He was very serious, though. Pierre can be devastating at any time, but in evening dress amid the warm scents of a Japanese garden, he's absolutely dangerous.'

In spite of the thirst-quenching properties of the melon, Annabel's throat was strangely dry. She gazed across the table at her tantalizing companion and endeavoured to change the subject to a less painful one.

'Are you appearing at the club this evening, because Aunt Bea is having friends to call and we're all going out to the fête in the town. It would be nice if you came too. You would enjoy it.'

'I'm not sure. Delia, the singer whose place I filled, might be well enough to return tonight.'

'Will you be sorry?'

Marilyn shrugged. 'Maybe. It would be a different thing if I had to work for a living. Why are you smiling?'

Annabel said, 'I was thinking how nice and easy life must be for you when you can shrug off a chance of a successful career without a pang. Do you realise that you have everything, good health, beauty, doting parents, wealth and ... success?' She had almost added, 'And Pierre,' but drew back the word in time.

'Do you think I ought to pursue a career?'

'I don't know what you want from life, so I can't advise you.'

'What do you want from life, Annabel?'

'A happy and successful marriage like that of my parents. They adore each other.'

There were dreams in her eyes at which Marilyn openly scoffed.

'You really do go for this love thing, don't you?'

Aunt Bea appeared at that moment to take her seat at the table.

'Hello, my dears,' she said. 'What are you both doing this afternoon?'

'I was going to ask Annabel to go shopping with me this afternoon to buy a couple of evening dresses for the show tonight,' Marilyn told her.

'But you're not sure you'll be going,' Annabel said.

'What of it? It's fun buying new clothes, and evening dresses are never wasted. I saw a gorgeous dress in a salon in Tokyo the other day, just the thing for tonight.'

Aunt Bea looked relieved. 'That's settled, then. By the way, Marilyn, a party of us are going out this evening, so do come with us if you aren't needed at the club.'

Marilyn promised, and after a few pleasantries, Bea went to her study.

The two girls spent a pleasant afternoon in the more exclusive shops in Tokyo. Marilyn got the dress she had seen, a halter-necked, figure-hugging model in pale blue and apricot. She also bought one in black and silver and a mink evening stole. Mink, she said, was cheaper in Japan than in the States.

Annabel wandered happily among a selection of kimonos, obis and happi coats. The latter were the feminine equivalent of the long blouses worn by Japanese workmen. Beautifully tailored, they ranged from delicate sunset colours to more exotic designs. Annabel bought several, including one for her mother and a more masculine one for her father.

They were busily putting their purchases in the boot of the car when Annabel suddenly missed Marilyn. Then she saw her across the other side of the road. She had reached the centre of the pavement outside the shops when a young man who had been leaning negligently in a shop doorway came forward and jostled her as he passed on.

Annabel, pushing back her hair from a hot forehead, tried to catch a glimpse of his face as he lost himself in the crowd. He was no one she knew. Marilyn still stood in the centre of the pavement and slowly she turned. Waiting for a break in the traffic, she came swiftly back across the road as Annabel closed the car boot.

Her smile as she arrived somewhat breathless at the car was easy and relaxed.

'Sorry about that,' she said. 'I thought I saw someone I knew across the street. There was no time to say anything, so I ran across the road.'

Annabel regarded her for a moment or two, entirely disarmed by the smile. 'And was it someone you knew?'

'No.' Marilyn's laugh did not ring true. 'I was mistaken.'

The sun was fierce, beating down like a branding iron on bare flesh. Annabel began to walk round to the side of the car, wiping the moist palms of her hands against her dress and feeling strangely cold inside. The whole incident had been so obvious, so unexpected that she might have believed it had not happened, except for one disturbing fact. Marilyn had been clutching her handbag with white knuckles.

Did she actually cross the road thinking she had

seen one of the group? But the man jostling against her had seemed deliberately to make way for her. Yet they had not spoken, for their lips had not moved, neither had they looked at each other. And he had not taken her handbag, for she still had it.

On the way back to her aunt's house, she tried to convince herself that Marilyn had spoken the truth. When they reached the house Annabel had almost convinced herself that she had been trying to make something out of nothing.

CHAPTER SEVEN

MARILYN did have to go to the Cherry Tree Club that evening. A phone call verified the fact that the group's singer was still indisposed. She came into Annabel's room before leaving for the club, wearing the apricot and blue dress and with diamonds at her neck and ears. Her beautifully smooth, tanned shoulders gleamed like satin above the halter neckline and she carried the new mink stole on her arm.

Annabel imagined dozens more like it languishing in Marilyn's wardrobes back home. The diamonds, she thought wryly, were definitely the real thing. They echoed the living sparkle in her eyes. Yet the only thing I really envy her is Pierre, she told herself sadly.

'You look ravishing,' she told her without rancour. 'Good luck.'

Marilyn smiled with less of her usual assurance. 'Thanks—I'll need it. Have a nice evening. I must fly!'

She sped away on a wave of expensive perfume. Annabel could still identify it in the corridor when she went downstairs to join her aunt, who was waiting for her friends to arrive.

'Sensible girl,' was her comment as she observed the French navy trouser suit and the accompanying white chunky-knit jacket her niece carried on her arm. 'The nights are apt to go a little chilly if you're out too long, especially in the hills.'

They came in three cars, a crammed-in, laughing, chattering group who spilled out to be introduced and take a drink before setting off. A mixed bag of English settlers, they acknowledged Annabel politely, obviously approved by their warm friendliness, and greeted Deno with a muted cheer when he arrived on the scene with a tray of drinks.

The two cars slid to rest behind the others so silently that only Annabel was aware of their arrival. The built-in radar which connected her to Pierre was sending out signals before she saw him extricate his length from his car. With mixed feelings she saw her aunt go forward to greet him and John, who was striding forward eagerly to meet her.

Laughing introductions all round gave Annabel the opportunity to see that all the guests were now paired off, her aunt with John and herself with Pierre. Then Pierre was standing beside her, drink in hand. She found herself breathing with difficulty and gripping her drink in the manner of one hanging on to a lifeline. She felt him watching her—and watching her with some amusement. It rankled. She wanted to ask him why he was not at the Cherry Tree Club.

Instead, she said, 'I never expected to see you here this evening.'

He raised a tantalising brow. 'And why not?'

'Because ...' Annabel found a difficulty in meeting his teasing regard and stumbled on, 'Because I expected you to be at the Cherry Tree Club with Marilyn.'

His dark eyes, quietly steady, rested unwaveringly on her flushed face.

'I might have been had John not rung me to ask if I cared to accompany the younger Miss Stacey on an evening out.'

'So you were hooked as a reluctant companion for the younger Miss Stacey. Thanks!' Pride put an odd note in her voice. Her slim straight back was held even more erect. It was very difficult to keep the tears from her eyes.

'*Touché*. Would you have preferred me to go to the Cherry Tree Club?'

Amusement was written plainly on his face.

'Naturally,' she answered stiffly. 'If you'd already made arrangements to see Marilyn it wasn't very sporting of you to let her down. I had no idea you'd been invited.'

Her voice, low with anger or disappointment, she was not sure which, was meant for his ears alone. She had spoken beneath the light-hearted laughter and chatter surrounding them, but immediately the words were spoken she would have given anything to withdraw them. What had got into her? Did she not know by now that Pierre was just not capable of doing anything unsporting or underhand in any way? Yet she had deliberately accused him of it.

Common sense told her to relax and take things easy. Far better to establish a relationship of friendship between them, one that would have all the outward appearances of the casualness of old friends.

Pierre did not move a muscle. Quietly, almost gently, he said, 'Do you want me to leave and go to the Cherry Tree? If I do so I can assure you that

113

Marilyn will be very surprised to see me, since I have made no arrangements to see her there or anywhere else this evening. Actually, I had just arrived back at my hotel after being out at a conference of journalists and had made no arrangements for the evening when John rang me up.'

Annabel was forced to meet his eyes. In them she saw no resentment at her implied insult. She was bitterly ashamed.

'I'm sorry, I shouldn't have said what I did. You see, my aunt has it in her head that I must be entertained every moment I'm here when I'm never desirous of having company pushed upon me. I'm perfectly capable of enjoying myself in my own way.'

He was looking down at her, his face oddly gentle. He was so strong, so clear-cut, so clear-thinking. He held life completely where he wanted it under his strong thumb. How could she ever hope for his understanding, his love? He who lived and loved and rode away to live and love another day.

'Your aunt wants the best possible time for you while you are here? I see nothing wrong in that, because I do too.' He smiled. 'Relax, *ma petite*, and enjoy what the gods offer. How is Marilyn?'

'On top form and looking very lovely when she left for the club.'

Annabel trembled at a question which could mean a lot or a little. He was studying the golden liquid in the glass he held in strong brown fingers.

'She is quite a girl,' he murmured as though his thoughts were miles away.

The fête was held in one of Tokyo's big parks made gay with stalls selling dolls, candy floss, postcards, funny hats, seafood, sweets, cookies, rice crackers and seaweed biscuits. They went the round of the stalls joining in the fun. Then they visited a shrine where they bowed three times, threw coins behind an iron grille and after clapping their hands twice, bought a candle to light.

The Shinto faith reminded Annabel of the Salvation Army back home. It was the same lighthearted, frank and open religion with no ponderous incantations. Prayers were offered with childlike simplicity with no false hypocrisy or lamentations of repentance.

Lighthearted and in the best of spirits, they reached a teahouse at the foot of the wooded hills. At a spring outside they washed their hands, left their shoes at the door and entered to sit down on tatami mats covering the wooden floor. The pretty girl in a jade kimono who served them green tea in bowls and rice cakes was as refreshing as the service she performed so graciously. Her hair arranged high on her head in natural wisps and curls framed a smile of utter sweetness.

Later they collected their shoes and left the building to walk to the path leading up into the hills. The trees they passed under were tinged by the orange flame of the setting sun. Annabel's eyes were directed to glimpses of the lake between them gleaming like molten metal. It was then that she saw him, the sallow face and small eyes set too close together, the furtive walk and the unbelievable swiftness with which he moved like an ominous shadow between the trees.

There was no mistaking him. It was the young man she had seen lounging in the shop doorway that afternoon when Marilyn had run across the road, the one who had jostled against her as she stopped on the pavement. She stopped to watch him, her mind instantly alerted, her heart beating with a strange frightened excitement.

Suddenly his form had closed in like a dark shadow

against a tree. The next moment he had gone, vanished as though he had been spirited away on the breeze. Annabel blinked, her eyes pierced the gloom, but he was no longer there. She had seen nothing happen, yet she knew something had. The tree, a very old one, squat and arthritic in shape among the more healthy ones, had been the object of his meandering. Memorising it, Annabel went on to join the others.

'Enjoying it?'

Aunt Bea spoke softly at her side. John and Pierre were walking ahead talking together.

'Very much.' She put on her white woolly jacket, feeling the keenness in the air upon reaching the shade.

Bea helped her, pulling up the back of her collar warmly around her neck.

'We're going to the summit of the mountain to watch the moon come up over Mount Fujiyama in the distance. It's something everyone enjoys when they visit the fête,' she said.

At the foot of the slope the party split up to walk behind each other. John stepped back to allow Bea to walk in front of him and Pierre did the same with Annabel. The climb was not a stiff one, although Annabel found herself wishing that it was. Pierre's protectiveness, his hands around her slender waist when he swung her up over grass-covered rock was a bittersweet torment. It was unbelievable that they should seem so close when they were poles apart.

At the top of the slope there was a rest-house with a veranda covered with tatami mats. A couple of Japanese students sat at one end, but there was room for a dozen or so more to sit in comfort and admire the view. They all sat down and Annabel found herself between Pierre and her aunt.

116

It was a beautifully clear night with the heat of the day tempered by the cool mountain atmosphere. The sky was a darkening blue and the voices of other climbers echoed up the slopes between blue-green pines.

Down below dove-coloured house tops looked mellow and serene between the glow of lighted stone lanterns in gardens. All was quiet up there in another world with Pierre. He had handed cigarettes round and they were sitting in comtemplative mood in the cool dewy air for something to reward them for their climb.

Annabel had accepted a cigarette but was not finding it too enjoyable. Pierre was much too close, and nonchalant, sending out a line of smoke carefully and lazily away from her. She started slightly when she felt his hand seek and cover her left one as it rested on the tatami mat between them. His warm fingers curling around it seemed loaded with electricity. She willed herself to endure it, knowing he was totally unaware of the havoc his touch brought to her whole being.

'Warm enough, *chérie*?' he murmured. 'Your hand is cold.'

'Yes, thanks,' she answered quietly.

In a maze of unhappiness and pain, Annabel listened to the quiet murmurings of her aunt and John who were intimately together, and she felt a fearful loneliness of spirit. Pierre's closeness, his deep, quiet voice, his dark teasing eyes and the long brown fingers curled with deceptive lightness around his cigarette awoke in her a longing which she knew had to be conquered if she wanted peace of mind.

Fiercely she told herself that the only reason he was with her, with time and leisure to pick up their acquaintance where they had left off, was because Marilyn was there in Japan.

'You are very quiet,' he said, looking down at her.

She forced herself to face reality. 'It's the witching hour.' She smiled up at him, relieved at the lightness of her tone. 'Is it a new moon we're waiting for? We English usually turn our money over for luck at the first glimpse of a new moon.'

He had turned slowly to see her more fully. His mouth twitched with amusement. 'And did you wish upon this new moon, *ma bien-aimée*?' he asked mockingly.

'Why, yes.' She was laughing now, her eyes full of dreams. 'Sometimes the wish came true.'

'*Mais vraiment*, I cannot believe it!' He was laughing now. 'I shall have to try this game of wishing on the moon.'

Suddenly shy of his intent regard, Annabel shifted her gaze to see the large waxen ball of the moon come slowly into view. She stared at its blue eyes wide, pink lips parted showing small white, even teeth.

'See, there it is—a lovely full moon. We can't wish on it, though.'

But Pierre had not turned his head to look at the moon, his unwavering glance was still on her animated face. She turned to look at him and their eyes clung. His expression now was sardonic, almost grim.

He quoted mockingly, 'A dreamer dreaming universes into being...'

Her voice was a husky whisper. 'And then dreaming them to an end only to start dreaming them again,' she finished for him. 'Alexander Campbell said that in his book *The Heart of Japan*.'

'So he did.'

She tore her gaze away with an effort. 'You haven't looked at the moon,' she accused him.

118

'I prefer to study the stars in your eyes. What a dreamer you are!'

Her eyes flashed blue fire and she looked at him, withdrawing her hand from his.

'And what a cynic you are, Pierre! Take your feet off the ground and join me in orbit, dream for a while. Or would you find that impossible?'

He looked down at her for so long, she felt her cheeks hot in the cool night air.

'You would be surprised what I can do,' was the cool reply. 'However, in this realistic world, *mon enfant*, one can easily be trapped during those moments of dreaming.'

'I don't know what you mean,' she whispered.

'There is an old Japanese proverb which says, and I quote, "Choose a bride and piece goods in the day-time".'

'You've made your point.' Annabel looked down at her half-finished cigarette and jabbed the end, ash and all, on to a flat stone within reach of the tip of the tatami mat. Then she looked up with a smile which she hoped reached her eyes. 'I suppose the same goes for choosing a husband.'

Pierre tossed the end of his cigarette, already squashed between his finger and thumb, way out in the darkness. She watched his dark profile, firm and resolute, and wondered painfully whether he was remembering the awful night in Paris when she had told him she loved him. He had scoffed then about the glamour of the evening blinding one to reality. His face then was much the same as it was now, only he had been gentle and kind. Now the kindness was tinctured with mockery, a hard mockery as if the last two years had not been too easy for him either.

How she hated the sense of humiliation the memory

of Paris conjured up! Was it possible that despite his full life and exciting job Pierre had found the one woman who would be able to hold him down, whose father also spoke the same language as himself in the matter of journalism? She was thinking of Marilyn who had trodden a common ground with him in the manner of travel and experience, a sophisticated woman who not only had but could give him everything.

The moon had risen higher, shedding her waxen light over the shadowy hills. In the distance Mount Fujiyama stood in isolated grandeur, hard and unyielding as Pierre, whose thoughts appeared to be miles away, she thought wearily.

'Coffee, honourable ladies.'

Annabel started to see a smiling young man clad in a white jacket over dark slacks hovering above her aunt with a tray of coffee. They all accepted it gratefully and Pierre fished some paper money from his pocket to place upon the tray.

The moon sprayed everywhere in a cold clear light when they all trooped down the slopes again, refreshed and warmed through with the coffee and their experience of being on top of the world. On reaching the bottom of the slopes, they all meandered to a little temple in the park, passing as they did so the small spinney of trees where Annabel had seen the young man of the afternoon behaving so furtively.

It was deserted now and looked ominously still and ghost like in the cold shafts of moonlight pushing through the branches of the trees. Annabel hung behind the rest of the party, seeing that Pierre was immersed in talk with her aunt and John as they neared the temple. She simply had to go to the tree where the young man had disappeared. What she expected to find there was not quite clear. But old trees did have recesses in the old bark in which one could secrete notes or ... even packages. The latter thought, coming all unbidden, smote her as a possibility—a frightening possibility.

She flitted silently across the grass, to pause a few feet away from the old gnarled tree, with an exciting expectancy, her heart beating in slow heavy strokes. The voices of her party were silenced on entering the old temple and she was alone among the trees, shadowy and mysterious in the moonlight. The slightest sound was amplified by the utter stillness, for the fête was on the far side of the park, the sounds muted and seemingly far away.

Her body grew tense and when the sudden movement of whispering leaves in a nearby tree startled her, Annabel gazed up at it fearfully. The next moment a hand was placed firmly in the small of her back and she was pushed forward violently. Taken unawares and unable to stop herself, she hurtled towards the old tree like a battering ram. As she struck the tree her head seemed to disintegrate into thousands of stars before blackness engulfed her.

A faint pleasant aroma of tobacco mingled with a masculine fragrance alerted her senses slowly. She opened her eyes slowly to gaze into the dark concerned gaze of Pierre. He sat against the tree and she was half lying across his knees in his arms. She raised a trembling hand to her head.

'No, do not move yet, *ma chère. Doucement*, take it easy.'

It was heaven to obey his command, to sink back with unutterable rapture into the beloved arms. Her head was throbbing unmercifully, but she would have endured that and more for the utter sense of peace and pure bliss just being held close to his heart meant to her.

'I'll ... be all right in a moment,' she whispered, as her memory returned.

'*Pauvre enfant*!' His voice sounded oddly unlike him. His mouth seemed to be buried in her hair. Once again Annabel felt the world spinning around her. She had surfaced from a sea of pain to be plunged into the more turbulent waters of passion and an unbearable need. The heavy beating of her heart threatened to choke her. The pressure of his arms became unbearable.

'I ... must have slipped on the dewy grass and plunged headlong into the tree,' she said, conjuring up a pale smile as she opened her eyes.

Pierre lifted his head to digest her words as though they were quite an unsubstantial statement.

'What were you doing here in the first place, straying away from the rest of the party?' He was frowning heavily as if unsatisfied with her explanation. His arms slackened around her. His voice demanded an answer.

'I ... I ...' Her look was piteous, and he became suddenly gentle.

He cut in on her stammer. 'I know what you are going to say,' he whispered. His face was in the shadow, but she saw the white charm of his smile banish the frown as if it had never been. 'You were enchanted by the moonlight and were looking for fairies and wondering if they existed in Japan.'

She clenched her nervous quivering hands. 'You're laughing at me again!'

He regarded her soberly for a long moment, the old derisive lines wholly gone from his face.

'I had never felt less like laughing in my life when I picked you up unconscious, not knowing what had happened to you,' he said grimly.

122

'I'm sorry.'

'You are not safe to be left on your own. Do you know you owe your life to the fact that the tree is an old one? Had the bark not been loose and cushiony with age you could have cracked your skull right open.' His voice had thickened and she was sure he was not aware that his arms had tightened convulsively around her. 'As it is, you have an outsize lump on your head and the skin is not broken!'

Annabel fought the pain in her head coupled with a ridiculous desire to burst into tears. In the silence which followed she felt him very gently removing bits of bark adhering to her hair. She dared not look up at him, but she could imagine his brown face set in grimly resolute lines giving no indication of his true feelings.

Her heart was beating so madly against him he must have felt it. A sense of pride gave her some semblance of control. Her voice was tremulous.

'I'm feeling much better now. Aunt Bea will be wondering where we are. She's sure to miss us.' She looked no higher than his brown throat. 'We'd better go.'

'Stop fretting, *ma bien-aimée*. If we are missed it will be assumed that we have gone off somewhere on our own. You, *ma petite*, are going home and are having the doctor.'

'Please, Pierre, I don't need a doctor.' She caught his sleeve. 'The skin isn't broken, so I don't require stitches. I'll be fine.'

'So you are fine. We shall see.' He scooped her up easily and set her down gently on the grass beside him. Then in one fluid movement he was on his feet, gazing down at her larger than life. 'Now we shall see.'

He made no attempt to help her up, but held out

his hands. Annabel reached for them and he pulled her up on her feet. The effort of rising sent excruciating pains in her head. She felt sick and ill and half dazed, not daring to let go of his hands.

Pierre stood, very steady, very quiet, looking down at her. 'So you feel fine?'

Annabel tried to answer him and wished everything would stop going round. But all she could do was hang on to his strong grip without uttering a word. At last she managed to articulate:

'I'm sorry. If you'll wait for a moment while I pull myself together . . .'

Pierre drew a rasping breath, swung her up into his arms and bore her away. Yielding to the inevitable, Annabel linked her hands loosely around his neck and suddenly felt spent. Letting her throbbing head fall against his shoulder, she closed her eyes.

The journey in his car back to her aunt's house was accomplished swiftly, although Annabel had only a hazy recollection of it. Pierre had carried her up to her room past the astonished, concerned gaze of Deno, who was ordered curtly to ring for the doctor. When Pierre had left her after lowering her gently on her bed to go to meet the doctor, Annabel managed to undress herself in between spells of sitting on the bed and slide into her pyjamas. It was heaven to lie back against the cool pillows.

The doctor came in a surprisingly short time. He was Japanese, young, efficient and very good-looking. 'Slight concussion,' he told Pierre in precise clipped English. 'Complete rest in bed for at least two days.'

When he had gone Pierre was bending over her with a half tumbler of water and two pills which the doctor had left to ease the pain in her head and help her to sleep. Sliding a strong arm beneath her, Pierre lifted her slowly and gave her the glass.

The door had hardly closed behind him before Annabel was asleep.

CHAPTER EIGHT

AUNT BEA was the first person to see her the following morning after Deno had brought an early cup of tea. Uninterrupted sleep had banished the pain from her head, leaving a woolly feeling and a sensation of having dreamed the events of the previous evening. However, the lump on her head was there to prove it had really happened.

Deno must have told her aunt that Annabel was awake, for she came bustling in, looking charmingly dishevelled in her dressing gown, to kiss her pale cheek.

'Poor darling!' she exclaimed. 'How are you feeling?' She sat down on the bed looking very concerned.

Annabel pushed herself up in bed and smiled wanly. 'I'm perfectly all right. Don't worry.' Leaning forward, she placed a hand over her aunt's resting on the bed and squeezed it reassuringly. 'It was only a bump on the head.'

Her aunt was unconvinced. 'Pierre said the doctor had ordered you to stay in bed. You have slight concussion.'

Annabel made light of it. 'Any bump on the head carries with it the threat of concussion providing it's severe enough. I didn't break the skin and I didn't have to have any stitches in it. I have a lump there, that's all.' She bent her head and indicated the spot. 'There, you see?'

Bea leaned forward and parted the dark hair gently. 'Good thing your hair is so luxuriant,' she said. 'What I can't understand is why you went off with Pierre. I kept with John in the temple and when we looked round both you and Pierre were missing.'

Annabel sat back on her pillows silently blessing Pierre, who on finding her missing had gone in search of her without mentioning it to her aunt.

'I'm sorry, Aunt Bea, but the park was so enchanting in the moonlight.'

'Was it indeed?' Aunt Bea looked down and stroked the tassel of her dressing gown thoughtfully. 'I think I ought to tell you that Pierre stayed until very late last night after waiting for me to come home. John dropped me at the door and wouldn't come in for a drink, so Pierre and I were alone.' She raised eyes which were curiously sympathetic. 'He talked mostly about Marilyn and asked how long she had known Kim and all about her. He's definitely interested in her, my pet. He's also a very charming man, devastatingly so. I would hate you to be hurt.'

Annabel managed a smile. 'Dear Aunt Bea! You're forgetting you enlisted my help in bringing Pierre and Marilyn together. I can assure you that Pierre's interest in me stems from the fact that he knows my parents. He regards himself as a big brother who feels it his duty to keep an eye on me while I'm here.'

Annabel waited for the gist of what she had said to register with her aunt, at the same time realising that Marilyn was inadvertently the cause of the bump on her head. Had she not seen the man jostle her on the pavement that afternoon so furtively, she would never have spared him a second glance on seeing him later in the park.

One way or another Marilyn had caused both herself and her aunt a lot of inconvenience. While she did not feel bitter with the American girl over her conquest of Pierre, she was bitter about the way she was ruining her holiday.

'Frankly,' she added before her aunt could speak, 'I shall be more than glad to see the back of Marilyn so that we can have a little peace.'

'I second that wholeheartedly. Having you here hasn't been the same since she arrived.' Bea left the bed and walked slowly to the window and looked out in silence. Then she turned round to look at the gay sunlit room, thinking how sweet her niece looked in her pastel blue pyjamas and her neat dark hair. I want her to be happy, she thought. She's so loyal, so courageous, so kind.

She smiled suddenly at the wide-eyed blue gaze fixed upon her. 'You ought to be sporting that lovely figure of yours on the Costa Brava or Palm Beach instead of lying there in bed. Sorry you came?'

Annabel sat up indignantly, delighted to find she could make a sudden movement with no recurring pain in her head. All she felt was an empty dullness which somehow matched the feeling in her heart.

'Bless you, Aunt Bea! I wouldn't have missed seeing you again for the world. I shall enjoy staying in bed in this delightful room and catch up with my reading. And stop worrying about me!'

Aunt Bea sighed. 'I'll send Deno up with the English magazines and morning papers. He's very fond of you.'

'He is?' Annabel looked surprised. 'I like him too.'

'In his opinion you're a number one person, an *ichiban*. He also thinks you're very pretty for an English girl and that some man is going to be very lucky some day to marry you.'

127

Annabel laughed. 'Thanks, that's made my day!'

When her aunt had left the room, Annabel fell to wondering about her assailant of the previous evening. Whoever it was had not wanted her to get nearer to the tree to examine it. But why? Was something hidden there? If there had been she would never know now, because whatever it was would have been removed.

There was one way of possibly solving the mystery —by asking Marilyn who the man was who had jostled her on the street that day and watching her reaction. Then the answer came to her in a blinding flash. Drugs! Her assailant was a drug pedlar who had hidden drugs in the tree for some customer to pick up. That day he had jostled Marilyn he had passed on the drug to her. There was the other time, too, when Marilyn had left her saying she had forgotten her purse when they had been in the park. Had that been just another excuse to meet some drug pedlar? Oh no! Annabel could not bear to think about it.

She lay back on her pillow and closed her eyes, fretting against her inaction. Yet what could she do? Marilyn might not be taking the drug herself. She could be getting it for Kim.

Upon reflection, she decided to say nothing to Marilyn. If Pierre loved her and wanted her, even if she was taking drugs, he alone could save her. And she was what he wanted. Annabel loved him enough to want his happiness more than her own.

So when Marilyn came in to see her before lunch she said nothing. Marilyn brought with her two dozen red roses arranged beautifully in a vase.

'Good morning, Annabel,' she said. 'Pierre sent you these roses. Aren't they beautiful?'

Coming swiftly across the room with her graceful

stride, she placed the vase down on the bedside table. Annabel found herself looking at her with new interest. She positively glowed. Late hours, cigarette smoke and the stale atmosphere of the Cherry Tree Club had done nothing to dim the radiance of her eyes, her skin, her golden hair.

'Did ... you did say Pierre had sent them?' she asked on a mound of pain.

Marilyn came to sit down on the side of the bed. She was wearing a lemon silk trouser suit. There were gold bracelets on her arms and the sun frolicked in her golden hair. A golden girl in more ways than one, Annabel thought wistfully.

'Yes.' Marilyn smiled at her knowingly. 'What have you been up to? Pierre says you bumped your head against a tree—slipped and fell or something. Made it sound serious.' Her eyes glinted and narrowed. 'He wasn't chasing you or anything, was he?'

Annabel ignored the last question and said quietly, 'Did you see Pierre last evening?'

Marilyn laughed. 'Goodness, no! Everyone was in bed when I crept in. I was downstairs when his flowers arrived, so before I put them in water I rang him up to ask him to come to lunch.'

'You did say the flowers were for me?'

'Yes. But I knew he was coming to see you today— he said so on the card he sent with the flowers. So I asked him to come for lunch. He was coming this afternoon, which wouldn't have been convenient for me.'

'I don't understand,' Annabel said flatly.

'Well, it's such a lovely day. He can take me swimming this afternoon. I feel quite stale after being at the club all hours. You don't mind, do you?' Marilyn asked archly with the familiar disarming smile.

'Why should I? May I have the card Pierre sent to me with the flowers?' Annabel tried hard to keep her voice off ice. She was beginning to understand how utterly selfish and self-centred a spoiled little rich girl could be.

Marilyn made great play of pushing her red-tinted nails inside the large patch pockets of her trouser suit. Annabel was not deceived when she drew them out again without producing anything.

'That's odd—I could have sworn I put your card in my pocket. However, it isn't here.' She shrugged. 'Sorry about that, but there was nothing important on it. I'll look for it and send it up to you later.'

'Thanks, I would like to see it.'

Annabel looked soberly at her, but she was in no way abashed. 'Tell me about your night out with Pierre. At least you didn't get a black eye in your fall.'

But Annabel had not the heart to tell her more than the bare essentials, which was just as well, for Marilyn soon grew tired of hearing about anything which did not concern herself. She was soon chatting about her night at the club, another success so it seemed. She did not stay long because of changing for lunch and Pierre.

Deno brought up the magazines and newspapers and a tray of mid-morning refreshment. Putting the tray on the bedside table, he poured out a glass of iced fruit juice and gave it to Annabel with a smile.

'Anything you want, Miss Annabel, please to let me know,' he said after asking how she was feeling. 'Nothing too much trouble.'

She tried the fruit juice and found it wonderfully refreshing. 'This is super,' she said, and laughed at the puzzled expression on his face. 'I mean it is good.'

He nodded and smiled. 'Good,' he repeated and his

small dark eyes danced.

'Deno,' Annabel looked thoughtfully down into her glass, 'did you see a card with my flowers when they arrived this morning from Monsieur Pierre?'

'No, Miss Annabel. Miss Firbank came downstairs early for the morning post and she received the flowers. I will look for the card if it is lost.'

'I wouldn't say it was lost, but Miss Firbank seems to have mislaid it.' She smiled at him reassuringly. 'Never mind, you have enough to do with an extra guest for lunch. Miss Firbank will probably find it. It's not important.'

Of course it was not important. Yet Annabel felt strangely impelled to ask about it. For some strange reason she had the feeling that Marilyn was deliberately withholding the card. But why? Was she jealous?

When Deno had left the room Annabel tried to interest herself in the English papers and magazines, but time and again her eyes strayed to Pierre's roses and she longed for yet dreaded his arrival. Fortunately she would not meet him at lunch. She was having hers in her room.

She heard the slam of his car door when he arrived and felt the very atmosphere change. Why do I love him so much, she thought despairingly, when it's such a hopeless love?

It was after lunch when Pierre came to her room, followed by her aunt and Marilyn. He strode in with the easy arrogance and lissom grace which was characteristic of him, tossing a negligent glance at his flowers on the bedside table. He looked carelessly elegant in a pale tan suit moulded on his wide shoulders with military smartness.

Poor Annabel, who had braced herself for his coming, felt a pulse beating in her throat, restricting her breathing. But she managed a smile.

'How are you, *chérie*?' he asked, his inflection bright and rallying.

'Much better. Thanks for the flowers.'

He stood looking down at her, his hands thrust into his pockets.

'How is the head? Pain gone?'

She looked at the masculine wrist watch visible between the edge of his pocket and shirt cuff and loved it because it was part of him. 'Yes, thank goodness,' she answered without raising her eyes.

'And you feel fine?' Something strange in his tone made her lift her head. She looked for the sudden gleam of his smile, only to meet his sombre gaze. 'Yet you ate very little lunch?'

Annabel was aware of her aunt and Marilyn in the background and her colour rose beneath the three pairs of eyes. In the short silence which followed Marilyn stepped forward to thrust her arm possessively through Pierre's.

'Stop bullying the poor girl!' she commanded, looking up at him with a hint of coquetry. 'Just for that you can take me swimming this afternoon!'

Her eyes challenged him and he smiled down at her lazily. He evidently found her commandeering vastly amusing.

'I came to see Annabel, *chérie*,' he reminded her amiably.

'But Annabel will be glad to see the back of you. You're being too domineering for words. Besides, our invalid is enjoying her stay in bed. She told me she's going to catch up on some reading.'

Pierre's gaze was curious and a little surprised. He looked mockingly at Annabel. 'Annabel would only have you think she is enjoying being in bed in order that you will not feel compelled to stay with her.'

Aunt Bea spoke quietly behind them. 'It's far too nice to stay indoors, so if you two are going swimming perhaps you'll post some letters for me on the way. Come, Marilyn, I'll fetch them for you.'

They left the room and Pierre strolled to the window. Annabel gazed wistfully at the back of the well-shaped head and wide shoulders.

'I'm perfectly all right,' she said. 'This time tomorrow I shall be up and feeling normal again.'

'You are not to get up tomorrow. The doctor said two days' rest.' Suddenly he spun round to face her. He looked fed up in some way.

Annabel's feelings were mixed. She wanted to comfort him, but at the same time she wanted to shake him for putting his happiness into Marilyn's careless hands.

She forced a smile. 'All right, I promise to stay in bed until the doctor says I can get up. Now don't look so grim. I'm not ill and I'm not going to be ill.'

He squared his shoulders and gazed at her intently and she clasped her small tapering fingers together on the coverlet.

'And you are not going to tell me what really happened last night?' he asked at last.

'I've already told you what happened. I slipped, lost my balance and pitched into the tree.' Gathering her scattered wits about her, she managed to speak with perfect calm. 'Now please, Pierre, don't think any more about it.'

He strolled slowly back to the bed, picked up her wrist to find her pulse and fixed her wide eyes with a narrowed gaze.

'How did you sleep last night? No nightmares?'

'I slept well—I always do.'

Annabel was despairingly aware of her leaping pulse. His touch was electric and there was nothing she could do about it. To her dismay, he sat down on the side of the bed to face her. Then taking her hand in his he spoke gently with a half quizzical tenderness.

'Annabel, *chérie*, we are friends, are we not?'

She lowered her eyes to the strong brown hands obliterating her own small one. 'Yes, Pierre, we're friends.'

'And you would tell me if anything that happened here frightened you in any way?'

She forced a smile. 'I suppose so. But what could happen?'

Annabel lifted her eyes to give him a disarming smile. But there were tears behind it. She clung to the sweetness of the moment, loving his nearness. An unbearable urge to push her fingers through his dark crisp hair, to draw his head on her breast and tell him about the attack on her by the tree was fought down with a superhuman effort. Her love for him prevailed.

She could not hurt him. To tell him meant involving Marilyn, and his alert brain would not be long in concluding that the girl was already taking drugs herself. As it was, Marilyn might have resorted to them since her cabaret act at the club to give her the boost she needed. In that case, Pierre could cure her with his love and devotion.

Annabel lay back, willing calmness and a lightness of manner. 'Are you trying to frighten me, Pierre?'

His shrug was very French. 'It is only that I have your welfare and that of Marilyn at heart. You are both young and impulsive, and to the adventurous a strange country offers many new cults which are tempting. Another point—this is not England, so do not go around casually as though it is. You will be much safer in Marilyn's company at such times when your aunt cannot accompany you out.' The foreign intonation in his tone became more marked. 'Promise you will go with Marilyn whenever possible. She handles her car extremely well and is a cool and confident driver.'

Lost in the deep tones of his voice, the concern, Annabel did not grasp the real reason of his request right away. Then it percolated. His concern was not so much for herself as for Marilyn. He was jealous of Kim and he wanted a chaperone for Marilyn in order to prevent Kim from getting close.

Her head started to ache and the throbbing pushed tears behind her eyes. She controlled her voice with an effort.

'I see your point,' she whispered, withdrawing her hand from his as if she found his touch intolerable. 'I promise.'

The door was flung open in that moment to admit Marilyn complete with beach bag and Aunt Bea's letters for the post.

'Ready, Pierre?' she asked.

Aunt Bea had tea with Annabel. Apart from commenting upon John's visit the previous evening, her aunt tactfully shied away from any mention of her unfortunate experience in the park. Annabel was grateful, and marvelled at the almost uncanny link she had with her father's sister. They were far closer than any mother and daughter. It was amazing that her aunt had not discovered her love for Pierre. She wondered how long it would be before she did. Her holiday was becoming quite a fiasco!

Marilyn called in to see her when she came back

from her afternoon spent with Pierre. Tanned and exuberant, she flopped down on the bed and laughed with the sheer joy of living. She had had a wonderful time. After Pierre had called at his club to collect swimming gear, they had driven to a beautiful bay where girls dived for oysters.

'Pierre is a splendid swimmer,' she said. 'One of the girl divers got into difficulties on the sea bed and he dived down to bring her up. Everyone thought she was dead because she wasn't breathing. Pierre worked on her for ages before she came to. He was all of a sweat, poor poppet, and quite a hero.' Marilyn sighed. 'I adore him!'

Annabel tried not to think of the happy times she had spent with Pierre during her holiday in Paris.

'What about Kim? Have you given him up in favour of Pierre?' she asked.

Marilyn gave a start and touched her lips with the tip of a hand.

'Oh, goodness! That reminds me. I promised to go early to the club this evening to run through my numbers before the show. The group have been out this afternoon playing at a charity concert.' Slowly she rose to her feet to stretch her shapely arms luxuriously above her head. 'Everything seems to be happening at once. Life is much more exciting here than ever it was in the States. What do you think, Annabel.'

'Things certainly happen here,' Annabel said dryly. 'I never bumped headlong into a tree before.'

Marilyn laughed. 'Poor Annabel! When you're up and about again we must go out and have a good time. Did you know Don is crazy about you? He's always asking me when I'm going to bring you to the club.'

Annabel said firmly, 'Don isn't my type, Marilyn. Affairs are out. I want to see as much as I can while

I'm here. I haven't seen much of Japan.'

Marilyn eyed her thoughtfully. 'You haven't seen much of anything, have you?' she said.

And with that scathing remark, she left the room.

CHAPTER NINE

By teatime the following day, Annabel had more than enough of lying in bed. The doctor had called in the morning to say she could get up that evening for dinner if she wished.

If she wished, Annabel thought wryly, feeling she would go round the bend if she had to endure another day in bed. She had not slept at all well the previous night. She had been awake when Pierre brought Marilyn home from the club and had lain staring into the darkness until his car had gone.

The utter silence following his departure was only a whisper of what was to come, nights and days of life without him, longing for a sound of his deep voice with its charming inflection, for the touch of his strong brown hand and that vital presence which infused so much life into her whole being.

That morning he had phoned to ask how she was. The unexpected sound of his voice when she had lifted the receiver had caught her unawares and a fluttering in her throat had altered her voice, making it sound weak.

'Sure you are all right, *chérie*?' he had asked.

'Perfectly,' had been the cool answer as her voice gained strength.

His call had been brief and there was another two dozen roses delivered an hour later. The accompanying card was not in his writing. It had been written by the florist.

Marilyn had said nothing about the card she had mislaid which had come with his flowers the previous day. Not that it mattered. Annabel was weary of it all, and Pierre's fresh bouquet, broken up into half a dozen enchanting flower arrangements by Deno, mocked at her from every corner of the room.

Aunt Bea knocked on her door when she was dressing for dinner to ask if she felt up to coming downstairs.

'You shouldn't have bothered dressing,' she said, zipping up Annabel's cornflower blue silk dress with its delightful square neckline and full skirt. 'You could have come down in your dressing gown. There'll only be the two of us. Marilyn has gone to the club. We can have friends in another time.' She looked fondly at the small pale face and shadowed eyes. 'You won't want to stay up late in any case.'

'The way I feel now I don't care if I stay up all night. I'm tired of lying in bed.' Annabel made up her face lightly as she spoke, then smiled at her aunt in the mirror as she put white studs in her ears to match the white beaded necklace around her slim throat. 'You know what Grandma Stacey always said. Being off colour is no excuse for going around sloppily dressed. Life is too short.'

Bea nodded, and sighed. 'She was a wonderful woman. The older generation have a wealth of knowledge gleaned from experience which is so valuable to the young if only they would heed. But they don't until it's too late. By then the old folk have gone and the world is all the poorer for their passing.'

The two women had a very pleasant evening. After dinner, they listened to the record player in the lounge and at ten o'clock Bea packed her niece off to bed.

'Better to have a good night's sleep,' she said.

But the tranquil summer evening beckoned from Annabel's room window and on a sudden impulse she went downstairs again into the garden. All was quiet with the sky a dark blue backcloth for the black silhouettes of trees etched against it. Humidity rose, smelling of nocturnal growth and green crops. The coastline was a necklace of lights and across the bay fishing boats danced upon the water like fireflies in the scented dusk.

Annabel thrust her hands into the pockets of the woolly jacket she had slipped over her dress and lifting her face breathed in deeply, finding the tranquillity a balm to her restless spirit. At every step she took through that quiet little garden, she marvelled at a race of people who could create beauty from sheer poverty—a twig lovingly placed in a vase, stones selected with tender care and placed in streams, utter simplicity, turning everyday life into poetry.

Suddenly her heart leapt as the sound of a car rudely shattered her thoughts. She paused to listen and gave a sigh of relief to hear it pass by in the road beyond the gate. For a moment she thought it was Pierre bringing Marilyn home. They could be back any moment, and the thought spurred her on out of the gate and along the road in the direction of the beach.

It was an enchanting walk along the cool leafy lanes, to pass gardens lit softly by stone lanterns. Some of the more elegant gardens with their traditional archways and little streams decorated by tiny bridges were hidden behind high walls with tantalising glimpses of them through the carved wooden gates.

Reaching the sea wall, she leaned forward with her arms resting on it and allowed the peace to wash over her. It occurred to her as she closed her eyes that she had lost two days of her precious holiday in bed. The lump on her head had almost gone and, as Pierre had said, it might have been worse.

Pierre again, she thought despairingly. Would she ever be free of his tantalising image? Why could he not marry his Marilyn and go out of her life? It would be a mortal blow to her own happiness, but it was the only way to purge her soul free of him. Tearing him out of her heart would leave irreparable damage. On the other hand, it would be a clean break.

A curious feeling inside her suddenly alerted her senses, and she turned to see him strolling towards her. In the gloom, he looked taller and wider of shoulder in the white dinner jacket.

His look flashed over her; his voice was angry. '*Mon Dieu*!' he exclaimed. 'Are you seeking another blow on the head?'

'Pierre,' she gasped, 'there's no danger. How did you know I was here?'

'Deno saw you leave the garden,' he replied in clipped tones. 'He told me as I was about to leave after dropping Marilyn at the door.'

She said awkwardly, 'I had to come out. The night is so beautiful after two days in bed.' She felt him move close beside her at the wall. 'Please don't spoil my pleasure. I was enjoying it.'

'Until I arrived,' he said sardonically. 'I'm sorry if I spoil your enjoyment. I am beginning to make a habit of it. The last time I was dismissed to spend the afternoon with Marilyn.' He slanted her a glance with raised eyebrows. 'How is the head?'

Annabel sensed his coolness as being directed

against something or someone other than herself. Something had happened to provoke him. He had said he had dropped Marilyn off at the door of the house. Had he proposed and been turned down? She stared unseeingly across the bay where the slowly rising moon cast a silvery pathway across the water. The cold waxen light seemed at one with the cold chill in her heart.

'Fine, thanks,' she said through cold lips. Scarcely aware of what she was saying, she prattled on, 'I hate to think I've lost two days of my holiday in bed. There's so much I want to see of this wonderful country.'

'Then we must do something about it.' His deep tones held a more bantering note. Bending, he placed his arms along the top of the wall and gazed out to sea. 'You are right, it is a wonderful evening,' he commented as though he had just become aware of it. 'Look at that moon.' He straightened then in the manner of one remembering something important, and stood very close, so close that every nerve in her brain was signalling electric charges through her body. 'I cannot answer for you, but I find its spell much too lethal. What about strolling down to the village? I can wager there will still be a number of restaurants open with Welcome written across the grin of the proprietor.' He smiled down at her. 'Care to do down to see?'

'Why not?' she answered.

Casually, they strolled down to the moon-washed narrow winding streets, passing the little shop where tatami mats were made on the premises and the open-fronted fruit shop where, during the day, tempting luscious fruits were displayed along with tangy tubs of dried fish and vegetables. Next door to the post office

141

was a hardware shop and a Shinto hall, then a restaurant in a tiny courtyard of bonsai trees and coloured ribbons fluttering over the open entrance door.

Pierre laughed down at her. 'Shall we go in?'

Inside one had the choice of sitting at the polished counter or squatting Japanese fashion on a raised dais to dine from small tables. They chose the bar and ate portions of fresh fish fried delicately in batter while they waited. The chef's movements were calm and unhurried, his expression serene, yet with a gleam in his small eyes which suggested an ever-present sense of humour.

This was the real Japan, Annabel told herself. It was still there in all its simple, calm, beautiful dignity, another world away from the overcrowded noisy streets of the city. The hand-painted wall panels were mellow and faded, the oak beams with lanterns attached were suggestive of comfort and friendliness. Such tranquillity could not help but breed smiles— and they were there on the faces of the diners, the little Japanese couple on the dais eating from the low table, their kimonos gleaming with the soft silky glow which came from years of washing and tender care, the young couple who had decided to dine western style at the bar beside them.

Annabel, her mouth sweetly curved, turned to find Pierre's dark gaze with its half-mocking smile fixed upon her.

'Enjoying it, *chérie*?' he asked lightly.

She nodded, lifting sparkling eyes and red lips sweetly curved, and wished it would go on for ever, just Pierre and herself. She was happier than she had ever been on those beautiful moments stolen from time. Slowly she popped the last morsel of tempting food into her mouth and leisurely finished her drink until there was no further excuse to linger.

Pierre had left his seat to go to a bookstand near by. When he came back to where she was sitting he gave her a hand and presented a street plan of Tokyo.

'You will find this useful, but do not get any ideas of going out alone,' he told her forcibly.

As they strolled back to the house, he talked entertainingly of humorous little incidents which he had enjoyed since coming to Japan. His sense of humour was one of his most endearing qualities, Annabel thought achingly, when they reached the house all too soon.

'Hurry to bed,' he commanded crisply at the door. 'It's much too late for you to be up. Sleep well, *chérie*. Pleasant dreams.'

Annabel had entered the porch to shed her shoes when she heard his firm footsteps crunching on the gravel to his car. Deno met her in the hall waiting to lock up the house.

'Sorry I kept you up, Deno,' she said.

He broke into his full-faced smile and bowed majestically. 'Evening much too beautiful to waste. Walk completely enjoyable?'

Annabel met his dancing eyes. 'Most enjoyable, thanks,' she answered with a twinkle. She went upstairs thinking that the admirable Deno was not averse to a spot of matchmaking. Too bad that he was barking up the wrong tree, so to speak!

Had Pierre taken Marilyn for a walk he would not have left her so precipitately at the door. They would have kissed and lingered to make a date. Yet why shouldn't they? Both were free. My love for Pierre is something known only to myself, Annabel mused bitterly. No one knew anything about it, least of all Pierre from whom she had taken great pains to conceal it by naming a prospective bridegroom.

The air became more oppressive as the night progressed, bringing the strange hush which usually heralds an approaching storm. Annabel had not gone to sleep when it came swishing down on the garden like a hosepipe turned full on. The fierce downpour went on to lull her to sleep and she awoke to a newly minted day with the sun filling her room with golden light.

After breakfast, heat was drying the garden up rapidly, sending forth a tangy fresh smell of damp earth and flowers, when Annabel went out with her aunt in the car to visit friends. Since Marilyn was still in bed and likely to be there for some time, they left without seeing her.

'You'll like the Tomes,' Bea said, putting on speed when they tossed the narrow winding streets of the village behind them to take a hill. They topped the rise to see a panoramic view of the lovely bay where tiny islets and clumps of rocks decorated the blue water.

'As I was saying,' Aunt Bea went on as they rounded the headland, 'the Tomes are very sweet. Colonel Tomes has business interests here which require many visits over the years. Two years ago he and his wife sold their home in England and came here to retire.'

She swung the car off the main road to glide along a broad avenue of trees and they travelled for some distance between pine woods. On either side bamboo, fresh, young and green, lightened the sombre background of giant trees.

The pine woods thinned out and another sweep to the left brought them to an entrance topped by a roof with pagoda-type corners provocatively curved upwards like the sweep of a coy maiden's eyelashes. They drove in past cherry trees to an enchanting garden where shrubs and flowers blossomed everywhere, against old walls, quaint summerhouses and reflected in a pool of lotus blossom.

Eagerly scanning the landscape, Annabel seemed to hold her breath as the car followed a bend in the drive to reveal the loveliest house she had ever seen. It was a mellowed residence crowned by the same type of picturesque curling roof over the gate. Behind it the wooded hills retreated into the blue sky while in front the sliding glass walls of the rooms seemed at one with the garden.

Aunt Bea drew up silently to the main entrance and both women turned their heads to see a tall gracious figure coming towards them across the lawns. She carried a long shallow basket in which lay freshly cut blooms and her gardening gloves. Annabel saw at once that she was middle-aged and had been very good-looking in her youth. Now the careful waves of hair were composed of more grey than brown, but her eyes were youthfully alert in the half-curious glance she turned upon Annabel.

'My dear Bea! How nice to see you,' she said with obvious pleasure as they left the car. There was no mistaking the warmth of their greeting as she looked curiously at Annnabel. 'You must be Anne's daughter. Those wonderful dark blue eyes could only belong to a Stacey.' She enfolded Annabel's hand warmly in her own. 'I went to school with your mother.' Her small laugh was pleasing. 'Gracious, it seems decades ago. Anyway, Anne has the better of me. I could never have produced so beautiful a daughter. You're staying to lunch—I insist.'

'Next to my own little house, I love yours, Olive,'

Bea said as their hostess walked with them indoors. In the wide cool hall, Annabel breathed in the indefinable scent of wood and the perfume of flowers. The beauty outdoors was repeated within as they entered a lounge to see the outer glass wall drawn open to the garden and a magnificent view.

Rich Chinese rugs in delicate colours covered the polished floor and the sunlight streaming in spilled on lacquer cabinets of collected treasures, flower arrangements on low tables and lovely old Japanese prints on the natural walls.

They were hardly seated when a houseboy, a classic study in black and white, came in pushing a small dinnerwagon of refreshments. He was followed by an elderly man who walked with military smartness. Colonel Tomes looked every inch a retired soldier, spare of figure, alert and lynx-eyed with the air of one accustomed to command. He came forward to greet them cordially, his grey eyes twinkling in his thin ascetic face.

'Welcome, Bea. This is an unexpected pleasure, especially as I'm now looking at you in a different guise,' he said heartily. 'I've just finished your last crime novel and I must congratulate you on being a master hand at suspense. I couldn't put it down.' He turned to his wife. 'You must read it, my dear. You'll find it a pleasant change from your light novels.'

His wife grinned sweetly. 'I'm sorry, but, with all due respect to Bea, I shall stick to my own little romances. And don't look so smug and cynical. More love is what this tired old world so badly needs. As you and I know, it's the only sound basis for a happy marriage. Why, look at this delightful child and dare to scoff at it.'

Annabel certainly looked enchanting in a cotton

146

dress the blue of which matched the colour of her eyes. The exquisite poise of her small head set like a flower on her slender neck above the picot-edged square neckline took the eye dramatically. In her small ears were white studs to match the narrow belt encircling her slender waist.

'Perfectly charming, and sweet of you to come, my dear,' he said appraisingly as they were introduced. 'Are you a writer too?'

Annabel shook her head. 'Aunt Bea is the clever one of the family,' she said lightly.

He nodded. 'It's enough for you to stand around and look decorative, eh?' His bushy grey eyebrows lifted quizzically. 'I know our other guest will agree with me.'

As if on cue voices were heard in the hall and the houseboy ushered in another guest. His wide shoulders seemed to fill the doorway. He wore an open-necked cream silk shirt and tailored pale grey slacks. Instantly, he filled the room with his strength of personality, conveying an almost primitive masculinity to poor Annabel, who all but dropped her cup at his sudden unexpected appearance.

Pierre, however, was in complete command of the situation. He smiled from one to the other with a tantalising elevation of his brows.

'*Mais vraiment*, I never expected to find three lovely Englishwomen waiting to receive me.' He bowed mockingly. '*Tiens*, I am overcome, and my pleasure is not a whit dimmed by the fact that I am already acquainted with the two delightful Miss Staceys.'

'Is that so?' The Colonel beamed with delight and his wife, obviously charmed by the newcomer, graciously offered him tea.

Without effort, Pierre impressed the French flavour of his personality by accepting the tea urbanely and Annabel, with the feeling of her heart laid bare for all to see, watched the nonchalant graceful poise of his body as he leaned against the lintel of the glass sliding door as though to isolate himself from too much personal contact.

'Oh, Pierre,' her heart cried despairingly, 'why do I have to keep seeing you?'

Yet, contrary to expectations, she found herself beginning to enjoy her impromptu visit. During the conversation she discovered that Pierre had made the acquaintance of the Colonel at his club in Tokyo and had been invited along to give his opinion on several pieces of beautiful porcelain which the Colonel had collected.

'These are certainly original pieces which were created during the Han dynasty in China,' he conceded, handling an exquisite vase in delicate blue green porcelain very carefully in strong brown fingers.

The Colonel's delight at the news, the warmth of the day and the beauty of the magnificent view from the lounge windows all combined to make it a morning fraught with pleasure.

Lunch was a crisp green salad, a great dish of it topped by prawns, chopped eggs, apple, celery, cress and nuts with Annabel's favourite salad cream. The latter was made from a Japanese recipe which Annabel was taking home with her after her holiday was over.

It was a gay meal and Pierre was so charming and amusing that Annabel saw with painful clearness how lethal his fascination was for someone as naïve as herself. Like herself, he was responsive to good food, new people, warm sun and friendly hospitality. But if he was lazily enjoying the restful, slow tempo of living

148

leisurely. Annabel found she could not altogether relax. She knew, and this frightened her a little, that the hold Pierre had upon her whole way of life created in her an insatiable need of something she knew not what. Silently she raged against her weakness and realised the futility of it.

They left soon after lunch, leaving Pierre and the Colonel going over more of his collection of objets d'art. On the way back in between light conversation with her aunt, Annabel told herself to be sensible, to pack up and go. Yet how could she? Cutting short her holiday for no apparent reason would only upset her aunt. She would be letting a beloved relative down, and she was not the type to let anyone down. Life would have to go on without Pierre and there was nothing to be gained by hurting others.

She must regard the incident in Paris, the heavenly time she spent there with him, as a closed chapter in her life. Finished. Maybe in the future she would look back on it without pain, but not now.

The next two days passed without incident and were peaceful without Pierre's disturbing presence. On the third day, however, Marilyn returned mid-afternoon from the Cherry Tree Club where she had been going through her evening numbers with Kim. It was to be her last performance as the resident singer was fully recovered from her illness and was to appear the following night.

Annabel had spent the afternoon on the veranda on a lounger reading and Deno had just brought tea when Marilyn arrived like a tornado. She flung down her handbag and sat down to give a splendid impression of an engine letting off steam.

'Kim is impossible!' she cried, her nostrils dilated

with temper. 'He demands perfection.'

Reasonably, Annabel said, 'You can't blame him for wanting to keep up the high standard he sets for the group. They wouldn't have been so successful in the past if he hadn't.'

Marilyn pouted mutinous lips. 'How can he expect a first-class performance from me when I go on in the evening completely exhausted from rehearsing earlier in the day? From now on he can go on without me. I've had enough!'

'But you have only one more evening. Tonight is the last, isn't it?'

'It was,' Marilyn lit a cigarette with hands which still trembled from her encounter with Kim, inhaled and blew out a line of smoke to watch it disintegrate. 'I shan't go this evening—I told him so.'

Annabel looked down at her paperback book thoughtfully.

'Isn't that rather mean? You haven't given him any time to find someone else. After all, it is for only one night.'

Marilyn looked indignant. 'After what he said to me? You ought to have heard what he called me!'

Annabel smiled tolerantly. 'I suppose you said some pretty unpalatable things to him too.'

Marilyn was unrepentant. 'Nothing that he didn't ask for. Who does he think he is anyway?'

'I gather that the idol has fallen from his pedestal. All the same, I don't agree in kicking the man when he's down,' Annabel said dryly.

The next ten minutes or so were taken up with Marilyn's account of what had occurred between herself and Kim. Listening, Annabel decided there were faults on both sides. However, she had nothing more to say and was relieved when Marilyn went to her room to rest and gargle her throat which, she said, would never be the same again after so much strain.

The silence when Marilyn had gone was decidedly restful and conducive to sleep. Annabel closed her eyes. Voices roused her, coming through the sliding glass doors of the lounge open to the veranda. Marilyn was on the phone talking to Don, the pianist of the group.

Annabel gazed out over the garden to watch large butterflies winging lethargically from flower to flower in the heat. Her aunt was in her study doing some typing before dinner that evening. Deno had taken her tea there. Still bemused with sleep, she was aware of Marilyn coming out to take the lounger near by. There was the rasp of her match as she lit a cigarette.

'Enjoyed your rest?' Annabel queried.

She turned her head to see Marilyn staring out unseeingly across the garden. Ignoring the question, she asked, 'Has Kim rung since I went to my room?'

'I didn't hear anyone. I've been asleep. Why?'

'Because that was Don on the phone. He says Kim isn't well and I ought to go to see him.'

'Could it be an attempt to persuade you to change your mind about tonight?'

'I don't know.'

'Was he well this afternoon?'

Marilyn shrugged. 'Hard to say. He hasn't looked well for some time.' She studied the glowing end of her cigarette. 'I suppose it is mean of me to walk out on him. But I'm not going tonight.'

'What are you going to do?'

'Go to see him. He might be ill.' Her eyes hardened at Annabel's smile. 'I can see you're expecting him to charm me back—but you don't know me.'

Annabel met her gaze squarely. 'No, I don't, do I?'

she agreed. 'And don't ask my advice. I refuse to influence you either way.'

There was a moment's silence with Marilyn smoking furiously. 'Would you care to come with me?' she
said at last.

Annabel hesitated. 'Wouldn't it be better to go on
your own?'

'I'd like your company. You could sit in the car
while I pop in to see Kim. He's at the club.' She
flicked a speck of tobacco from her lower lip. 'If you
go too I can always say we're going out to dine with
some friends of Aunt Bea's.'

Annabel looked down, almost abstractedly, at her
sun dress. She did not feel inclined to go in the least.
But Marilyn was unhappy or worried, there was no
telling really. There was no shaking off the feeling that
the girl was hiding something and it was this that
made her unwilling to co-operate. However, she
needed help and that was it.

Annabel shrugged off her forebodings and smiled at
her companion, feeling better for it. 'I suppose that
means we shall have to change.' She looked at her
watch. 'We have two hours to go there and back before dinner—if we change now.'

Marilyn stubbed out her cigarette. 'What about us
going on afterwards to Uncle's place? You know the
American Club Hotel?'

Annabel swung her legs off the lounger and looked
at her. 'You won't change your mind about appearing
at the Cherry Tree this evening?'

'No,' Marilyn said firmly. 'In any case, I've brought
my dresses home, so there'll be no question of it,' im-
patiently. 'Come on, let's go!'

'We'll have to tell Aunt Bea we won't be in to dinner.'

'I'll tell her,' said Marilyn.

The big car swallowed up the distance into town with Marilyn disinclined to talk. She appeared to be strung up and totally unlike herself. Annabel put it down to concern over Kim. From what she had learned already of the girl's character, she ought to have known better.

She noticed that they were approaching the Cherry Tree Club by a different route from the one Pierre had taken, enabling them to approach from the north end instead of the south. A wide entry allowed them to drive to the back premises of the club facing the courtyard entrance.

'I shan't be long,' Marilyn assured Annabel as she left the car. She glanced back before entering the courtyard to toss a smile, then disappeared.

It was very quiet after the noise and bustle of the city. The back entry seemed to be used solely by the inhabitants of the club and perhaps the staff of the cinema and public bath house on either side. Marilyn had been gone at least twenty minutes when Annabel heard the sound of music growing louder. She glanced towards the back entrance of the public bath house to see three youths emerging with a transistor set. They looked freshly scrubbed in kimonos with obis around their hips. In western clothes they would be attractive, slim young Asians. Now their kimonos had subtly transformed them. They looked more mature, dignified and wholly Japanese. They bowed and smiled as they passed the car, as though by simply donning the kimonos their whole demeanour had changed with them to the old-world courtesy so pleasing of their race.

Then Annabel forgot them when footsteps were heard coming from the courtyard. To her surprise it was not Marilyn who appeared but Don, the group's pianist. He seemed to be in a hurry. Opening the car door, he slid into the driving seat beside her and pressed the starter.

Annabel quelled a tremor of uneasiness. 'What's happened? Is Kim worse? Are we going for the doctor?'

She realised as soon as the words were out that had they needed the doctor they would have phoned him. But the long wait for Marilyn and the inner feeling that something was wrong had reduced her alertness to a sense of terror. Quickly she pulled herself together. What had she to be afraid of? It was daylight on a lovely summer evening and although they were travelling at a terrific rate there must be some plausible explanation.

At last she asked quite calmly, 'Would you mind telling me where we're going?'

Don did not turn his head. She noticed he wore evening dress and looked quite smart. But his profile was not reassuring. He was grinning.

'Relax, baby,' he said. 'You and I are having a night out.'

Annabel braced herself to meet this startling announcement with restrained anger. 'Stop kidding! A lady likes to be asked out for an evening, not kidnapped. I certainly don't care for your lack of manners —besides, you'll have to be back for the evening performance. You'd better take me back.'

The car leapt on and houses became fewer as they left the town behind. It seemed an age before Don answered.

'There's no show tonight, honey. The Cherry Tree is closing for a while for decoration.'

Annabel sat very still. 'Then ... Kim isn't ill.

There was no quarrel this afternoon between him and Marilyn?' she managed.

'There was a quarrel all right. That's what sparked the whole thing off. The idea was to close the club tonight after the show and start work on a new act while the place was being redecorated. When Marilyn walked out this afternoon Kim decided not to have an evening performance, and the manager agreed.'

Annabel began to feel a little easier. So Marilyn had not tricked her into coming with her. She was not to know what happened after she had walked out. Then she remembered the telephone call.

'What did you tell Marilyn on the phone to persuade her to come to the club?'

'Simply that Kim was ill and would like to see her.' He tossed her a guarded look. 'Why all the third degree? Stop biting that stiff English upper lip. Relax, honey. You can be good fun if you'll only let yourself go.'

Annabel sat stiffly beside him, uncertain how to act. She would get nowhere by repulsing him. He had evidently made plans of his own which he was determined to carry through, and she was part of them. He was driving far too quickly now, tossing farms, where mothers worked and children played beneath the shade of pawlonia trees, aside for lush fields from which humidity rose like steam.

The speed he had set up cooled the interior of the car and gradually Annabel became more alert. They shot through a village and she ventured to take stock of the landmarks when they turned inland between the hills where yellow tobacco leaves were drying in the sun and a brilliant bedspread hung to air over the balcony of a small brown house.

Don was slackening speed to drive along a road

overhung by trees leading to what appeared to be a garden tangled with weeds. Don stopped the car at the entrance, a pagoda-roofed gate high with weeds. He gestured beyond the gate.

'Behold the Temple of Love,' he said, grinning down at her with his arm sliding around the back of her seat. 'We shan't be disturbed here, baby.'

The next moment he had bent his head and was kissing her. Annabel could neither struggle nor cry out, for he held her in a vice. His hot lips filled her with nausea, but there was only one thing to do. She would have to play along with him instead of whipping up his passion by repulsing him.

When she could at last free her lips, she deliberately relaxed in his arms.

'I thought you Americans were more subtle in the art of making love. We have all the evening, you know, and you told me to relax. Why not do the same?'

Her quiet tones had their effect. Don's arms slackened and he laughed.

'Quite a girl, aren't you? I knew you weren't as demure as you pretended to be.' He looked at her with open admiration.

'Then why behave as if I had to be thawed out? Let's leave the car for a breath of air. It's hot in here. Besides, I want to see the temple.'

His eyes narrowed slightly, he appeared to hesitate. Then, to her relief, he smiled. 'O.K., baby. Anything you say.'

Annabel forced trembling legs to support her as she left the car to stroll as unconcernedly as possible towards the entrance leading to the temple. In the forecourt of the courtyard, arthritic limbs of old trees looked grotesque yet strangely dignified. The temple was beautifully carved. Annabel sensed the restful atmosphere as one of dignity and forbearance.

As they walked up the steps leading into the prayer hall two large-winged birds flew out disturbed by their approach. Startled, Annabel stepped back and felt Don's arm whip round her. Her shudder was not wholly on account of the birds.

Valiantly, she suffered his hold on her as he grinned down into her startled face.

'There's nothing to be afraid of,' he scoffed. 'I've been here before.'

'With other women?'

He shrugged. 'Why else would a guy want to come to a dead end like this?'

'To look at the temple, of course. Don't lovely old buildings mean anything to you?'

'Not when I've more enjoyable things on my mind!'

Annabel tried not to show her revulsion at his knowing wink and, gently sliding from his protective arm, ran lightly up the steps. On the threshold, she paused to allow her eyes to become accustomed to the dimness within until the feel of Don's shoulder behind her urged her forward.

At first she could see nothing in the gloom, then she saw hanging banners, dusty and faded, and an altar with wooden trays of fruit placed upon it. As she moved nearer, her heart lifted a little with relief.

'Someone must still use this temple,' she said. 'Look, the grapes are quite fresh and the apples. And here's a purification wand they use in the service.'

Annabel touched the streamers hanging from it, wondering feverishly whether the thing was heavy enough to knock Don out in order to make her escape. It was then she saw the porcelain saké jar in the shadowy recess by the altar.

Don drew level with her to take a closer look at the fruit and she gestured towards it.

'That saké jar—I saw a similar one the other day while visiting a friend of my aunt's. It was the same bluey-green shade and was said to be a collector's piece.'

Annabel held her breath as Don moved forward to bend over it. It was now or never, she thought desperately. Summoning all her strength to her aid, she raised her foot and planting it on his rear thrust him forward. His head hit the wooden wall with a dull thud and she was away, yanking up her long skirt in order not to impede her flight. Down the temple steps she flew with winged feet through the undergrowth of the courtyard to the car.

For one blood-chilling moment, she paused with her hand on the door handle. Had he locked it? She had been too distressed to notice earlier when they had left it. To her unbounded relief, the door opened to her desperate tug and she was inside. With her breath coming in painful gulps, she rapidly reversed the car, not daring to glance towards the temple.

She saw him as she successfully turned the car. He had staggered to the entrance gate and was shaking his head in an effort to clear it.

The sight of her in the car revived him and he lunged forward. But it was too late. Annabel had gone some distance before she was aware of the tears running down her face. I'm an idiot, she told herself, stopping the car at a safe distance to wipe them away. Then, blowing her nose, she cheered herself up because the wretched man had looked little the worse for her attack.

It had been common sense to get away, though. While he might not have done her any harm there was the risk of him taking drugs, in which case he could not have been responsible for his actions. Soberly she started the car and put on speed. He was not likely to get a lift for some time, for she had met no vehicle on the road since leaving him behind.

She concentrated on her driving, passing the familiar landmarks, the little brown house with the bright bedspread on the veranda and the yellow tobacco leaves drying in the evening sun. Then, leaving the foothills behind, she was soon cruising through the little village and on past the farm where the women were still labouring in the fields while their children played beneath the pawlonia trees.

It was on a sigh of relief that she turned eventually into the wide entry behind the Cherry Tree Club. But the place was closed, the back entrance door locked when she tried it. Back in the car, Annabel pondered over her next move. Marilyn would hardly have gone back minus the car to face Aunt Bea's awkward questions. If she could go back.

Annabel's blood ran cold at the thought that Marilyn might have walked unwittingly into a trap herself. Don could have been lying about Kim being ill. What if the man wanted to take his revenge upon Marilyn for walking out on him? The sensible thing to do was to go to the American Club Hotel. If she was not there perhaps her uncle would help in finding where she was.

Marilyn's uncle, looking every inch the successful proprietor of a plush hotel, was crossing the foyer to the lift when she entered. He smiled and waited for her to walk up to him.

'Good evening, Miss Stacey. If you're looking for Marilyn you'll find her in the cocktail lounge. I must go. See you later.'

He strode to the lift and Annabel joined a small party en route for an aperitif before dinner in the cocktail lounge. On the threshold of the room she paused to gaze around at the cosmopolitan crowd filling the bar and small tables.

Marilyn was sitting at the far end of the bar. Her golden hair was a shining halo around her head and her eyes sparkled no less brightly than the glass of champagne she held in her hand. Her full lips were smiling coquettishly up at Pierre. The diamond bracelet on her slender arm flashed fire as she lifted her drink to him in a silent toast.

Annabel stared dazedly as all sounds, the light laughter and chatter, the chinking of glasses receded. She might have been on a desert island for all the surroundings meant to her. At last she turned unsteadily, almost colliding with a couple going in. Concerned by her paleness, they stopped to ask if she felt all right. She nodded, hardly aware of them. All she could see was Marilyn and Pierre gazing into each other's eyes as if . . .

Somehow, Annabel made her way back to the car to sink weakly into the driving seat like someone recovering from an illness. A pulse beat unsteadily in her throat and her face in the driving mirror was ghastly. The relief at finding Marilyn safe and sound was swamped by her emotion on seeing her with Pierre.

Soberly checking that emotion, Annabel told herself severely that it was nothing to do with her. They were both free agents, free to choose their own life partners —which was presumably what they were doing in choosing each other.

It was a long time before she ventured to start the car. When she did so, she was quite composed, although her hand shook a little on pressing the starter.

Deno met her at the door.

'Miss Stacey had to go out,' he said. 'Dinner is about to be served.'

Annabel, who had never felt less like eating in her life, could not resist the silent appeal in his eyes not to waste the meal he had prepared for her aunt.

She gave in gracefully. 'Thank you, Deno. Miss Firbank won't be home yet. She's dining out.'

Annabel managed to eat enough of the carefully prepared meal to satisfy Deno before changing into a sweater and skirt for a walk before bed. She was back in her room preparing for bed when the phone rang. It was her aunt.

'Hello, Annabel,' she said. 'I shan't be back until late. John has suffered a sudden collapse. I'm with him at his club waiting for the doctor. It seems to be caused by exhaustion.'

'Oh, I am sorry! Is there anything I can do?'

'No, dear. I've put him to bed under protest, but I think he's enjoying the attention. Bye-bye. I shall be late home.'

Annabel slipped into bed after saying a prayer for John's recovery. There was a strong link between herself and John, she thought, for they both knew the merciless pangs of unrequited love. The tears came then.

CHAPTER TEN

THEY were in the dining room with the sliding glass doors closed to the light drizzle of rain shrouding the garden. Marilyn had not put in an appearance and the conversation during breakfast had been centred upon

161

John's sudden collapse the previous evening.

Annabel folded her table napkin, glad that the farce of eating was over. She was still numb from the events of the previous evening and refused a cigarette from her aunt.

'So John was all right last evening when you left him, Aunt Bea?' she said.

Bea exhaled smoke pleasurably. 'Yes. The doctor agreed that it was a collapse from sheer exhaustion of filling too many engagements in the heat. John has so many friends here and he's such a darling he finds it hard to resist their demands.'

'Is he going home?'

Annabel looked for some kind of emotion in the older woman's face at the question, but saw nothing only a tender smile.

'I've managed to persuade him to go. After the week's rest the doctor stipulated that, of course. As a matter of fact I've had a letter from his daughter saying how they miss him and how she's longing for him to come back so that she can show off her beautiful baby.'

Annabel said shrewdly, 'You don't think you're the reason he's stayed so long?'

'I know I am.' Bea shook her head sadly and flicked ash into a tray. 'I'm afraid it's no use, though. Had John been on his own with no one to care for him I wouldn't have been able to help myself. I would have had to marry him. As it is, he'll go back to his lovely estate and beautiful daughter to lead a full life, with the added interest of a grandchild and possibly more to come.' Her eyes suddenly narrowed at her niece's intent regard. 'I believe you're disappointed!'

Annabel's sweet lips curved into an impish smile. 'Romantic, that's me. I suppose I was hoping for a nice husband for my favourite aunt.'

'Your favourite aunt is quite happy as she is, thank you. What about you? I too would be wildly happy to know my favourite niece was settling down with a nice husband.'

The creases in the table napkin assumed the utmost importance as Annabel gave her attention to smoothing them out on the table with hands which had a tendency to tremble.

'There is someone who wants to marry me—Francis Kerrison. He's a Q.C. and a very clever one. He's very nice and awfully fond of me ...' She broke off, aware of her aunt listening intently. 'He's an only son with a mother I can't stand. By that I mean I don't love him enough to even try to like her.'

'Or marry him?' Her aunt nodded understandingly. 'You wouldn't be marrying his mother, you know. A deep friendship could culminate in a happy marriage. On the other hand, these sons of doting mothers can make appallingly selfish husbands.'

Annabel shone at her aunt. The shadows lifted momentarily from her deep blue eyes. 'Thanks very much. You have something there. I'm very grateful.'

'What for, my dear?'

'For helping me to make up my mind about Francis. I'd more or less promised to let him know on my return what I'd decided. I know now I can never marry him.' She stood the folded table napkin on the table and looked at it in satisfaction. 'That's Francis finished with!'

The napkin fell over and her aunt chuckled. 'I hope that isn't symbolic of how he'll take your final rejection. Poor man!' She crushed out her cigarette as the wall clock struck ten from the lounge. 'I must phone John—he's probably awake by now. The doctor gave him a sleeping draught.'

She turned as Deno appeared with a cable for Marilyn.

'I'll take it up to her,' said Annabel.

All was silent at Marilyn's door, but there was a sound of a drawer being closed hurriedly from within at her quiet knock. She was fully dressed and standing with her back to the dressing table to face the door when she bade Annabel come in. They stood staring at each other until Marilyn put on her usual disarming smile.

'Why, good morning, Annabel. How sweet you look! You should wear blue more often. It reflects charmingly in your eyes.'

'So they tell me. This cable came for you.'

Annabel's sober glance relegated the disarming smile to the depths where it belonged. She relinquished the cable to red-tipped fingers which shook as they tore it open.

'It's the parents!' Marilyn exclaimed on a happy note. 'This means I can keep my good news until they arrive.' Was her gesture of delight made with her left hand deliberate in order to display the magnificent solitaire on her engagement finger?

It seemed to Annabel to flash like a sword thrust in a mortal blow to her heart. Her lungs cried out for air.

'Do you mind if I open the window?' she managed.

'Go right ahead.'

Annabel opened the window and gulped in the sweet rainwashed air. Below, the garden sparkled in the sun. The rain had stopped for a brand new-minted day without Pierre.

Marilyn was chatting away happily. 'I wish you'd joined us last night. It was quite a celebration. Kim came, and Uncle was so disappointed because you didn't stay. What happened?'

Annabel folded her arms to clasp her elbows tightly in an effort to assuage the pain in her heart. She turned from the window.

'I was going to ask you that,' she said quietly.

'Were you?' Marilyn sounded genuinely surprised.

'What happened when you left me in the car at the Cherry Tree to go in to see Kim?'

Marilyn moistened full lips and spoke with a facetious lightness.

'Well, Don was there. They were packing up, you see, but Don has probably told you that. He wanted to take you out. You know he's crazy about you? I thought you'd enjoy it. I also thought you decided not to join us at the hotel because you couldn't tear yourself away from Don.'

'I had to tear myself away from him all right. I'd already done so when I arrived at the hotel. I didn't stay because I didn't want to butt in.'

'But that's ridiculous. We would have been delighted for you to join us. Uncle put on a special dinner for us later in the evening. Kim has moved into the hotel. The group are going back to the States.'

So that was it! Kim, shattered by Marilyn's engagement to Pierre, was packing up and going back home. Her engagement to Pierre had brought the whole painful chain of events to a cataclysmic end.

'I thought Kim was ill.' Annabel's voice was deadpan.

'He is. He's not been well. However, the rest will do him good. What happened between you and Don?'

Marilyn had changed the subject with lightning rapidity. Annabel took it in her stride, still not quite realising that she, the gentle romantic, had resorted to violence.

'We disagreed on how to spend our evening. I'm afraid I had to ram it home to him rather painfully.'

Marilyn giggled. 'What did you do? Come back here?'

'Yes.'

Marilyn sobered. 'Sorry about that, when you could have been having a good time with us at the hotel.' She put down the cable on the dressing table. 'I guess I shall have to go to air the house for the parents when they arrive. I shall have to round up the staff too.' She raised a dainty brow in query. 'Like to come with me?'

Annabel armed herself with a bright smile. 'I shall have to ask Aunt Bea if she's made any plans for to-day. I'd like to go with her to see John. He's leaving for home at the end of the week.'

She went on to tell Marilyn about his collapse, but all she received was a shrug. Marilyn was already immersed in thoughts of a future wedding.

'See you later, then,' she said.

Annabel nodded and left the room. She did go with her aunt to see John. He was in his dressing gown when he admitted them into his suite of rooms at his club.

'Charming of you to come, my dears,' he said, giving a wry grimace at the endless gifts of fruits, flowers and a coveted biography he had wanted which the two women placed on a table. 'You are darlings, you know, when I'm not really ill. And what's this?' Picking up the book, he gave a whistle. 'Six pounds fifty! I insist upon paying for this, Bea.'

'No.' Bea placed her hand over his as he held the book, and Annabel moved away. 'It's a farewell present from me. You were very kind in advising me technically with my last novel.'

'It was a pleasure—you know that.' He looked down at her for several seconds, then bent his head to kiss her gently on the lips. 'I shall be waiting in case you change your mind,' he told her gravely.

A sudden tap on the door drew them apart. John strode to open it to Pierre. He entered nonchalantly with that innate ease of manner which was so much part of his charm.

'I came to ask how you were. I've only just heard of your collapse last evening—I believe you had the doctor. I trust it is nothing serious, *mon ami*.'

John shrugged. 'It was the heat and burning the candle at both ends. I'm fine again. Nice of you to call. Come and make the number even.'

John drew Pierre forward and he saw Annabel and Bea. '*Enchanté*,' he exclaimed, his mocking gaze touching Bea before lingering upon Annabel, who began to feel hot beneath the white mackintosh she had slipped over her dress. 'I do not wonder at your swift recovery in such charming company.' He bowed. 'Good morning, Miss Stacey—Annabel.'

'Sit down, all of you,' invited John. 'Make yourselves comfortable while I pour drinks.'

'Allow me to do the honours, John.' Pierre pushed his host down gently into an armchair while Annabel and Bea sat down nearby on a sofa.

'Is it true that you're leaving next week, John?' Pierre strode to the drinks cabinet as he spoke.

'Quite true.'

As he answered, John leaned back in his chair and Annabel thought he looked tired and drawn. Then she looked across at Pierre and admired as always the quiet perfection of his clothes, the well-shaped head of crisp hair, the wide-shouldered figure tapering down to whipcord strength of physical wellbeing.

'I shall be leaving soon myself,' he said, manipulating bottles and glasses expertly in firm brown fingers.

'Another assignment, Pierre?' Bea asked when he brought her drink.

He laughed, his eyes full of a roguish raillery that twisted Annabel's heart. 'The most important assignment of my life—and do not ask me what it is!'

Annabel lowered her eyes from the dark tantalising face. He was evidently keeping his engagement to Marilyn a secret until her parents returned from the States. Well, at least she would be spared the ordeal of congratulating him. She doubted whether she could have gone through with it in any case.

She felt too choked for refreshment. 'No drink for me, Pierre, thanks,' she managed.

He turned slowly to look down at her, his eyes narrowing. '*Voyons, ma chère. Vite*—off with your coat! You are steaming beneath it.' Bending down, he gripped her upper arms and gently raised her to her feet. Then he peeled off the white mackintosh and laid it over a chair. 'You will now take refreshment, *ma jolie* Annabel, something to bring the colour to those wan cheeks. You also appear to have been too energetic in the heat.' He lowered her down again into her chair as he spoke and was away to the drinks cabinet. He was back in a trice, his look compelling, to hand her the glass. 'Here we are, a rich burgundy from my own country by a namesake of mine, Pierre Picard, to bring a sparkle to your eyes.'

Annabel lifted her head. It was inevitable. Their eyes met and locked. The fingers brushing her own as she took the glass were electric. In that moment—only for that moment—the mockery had gone from his eyes. Then, with a lightning movement, he had gone to fetch his own drink, leaving her feeling strangely shaken and very conscious of her aunt's smiling interest.

The wine warmed her cold heart, but when John offered his cigarette box, she refused and tried to assume a lightness she was far from feeling. Pierre, taking up a position with his back to the fireplace, stood carelessly at ease between his host and the two women. As he passed the table of gifts his keen eyes had rested upon the book Bea had bought and he viewed it with pleasure.

The conversation inevitably turned to books. Pierre, it seemed, was extraordinarily well read and shared John's delight in an original edition of *Les Chroniques des Pasquier* by Georges Duhamel which John had found in an old bookshop near the Ginza.

On the surface it was a happy informal little gathering which ended with John having lunch brought up to his rooms. Annabel, who had expected the visit to be a short one, gave in and made the best of it. During the meal it was Pierre who dominated it in a subtle way. His charm went beyond mere physical attraction. He had the tact and congenital ease of manner which experience of the world alone can impart. He was sympathetic and quick to understand, with the happy gift of setting those around him at their ease.

He was certainly good for John, drawing him out and not tiring him with too much talk. When Annabel and Bea took their leave of him he looked a little better and much brighter for their visit.

The rooms at the club did not provide the right background for John. Annabel could see him clearly on his country estate walking with a dog at his heels surrounded by faithful retainers. Her aunt would think the same, but how complete the picture would be with a wife at his side. Pity, they would have made an ideal couple.

After leaving John's club they drove into town to do some shopping. It was while they were having tea in a charming little English-style café that the clouds which had hovered in the hot air all day finally burst into a deluge. The sun had come out again when they resumed their journey home, after being pelted by drops from sodden trees when they made their way to the car park.

Annabel's head had begun to ache. In the sticky heat, she felt exhausted and depressed but grateful to her aunt for taking her out. Anything was better than staying indoors or going out with Marilyn. She had no desire to go out with Marilyn—it would be far too painful. Each time she looked at the girl she would see eyes that Pierre looked into and lips he had kissed.

Annabel could no longer summon up even the spurious comfort of self-pity. Life, as she now saw it, had no meaning for her. She glanced at her aunt, engrossed with her driving, feeling a little guilty at her obsessive love for Pierre, a love she could neither stop nor discuss with her.

At the same time Annabel was astonished that her aunt had not already perceived it. Two years ago she would not have missed it. It was shattering to discover that the strong sense of telepathy between them now seemed to be no more.

How to live through the rest of her holiday was a problem. When the Firbanks returned they would be so delighted to hear that their daughter's last link with Kim and his group had been severed that they would almost certainly insist upon the immediate announcement of her engagement to Pierre. The wedding would follow very quickly. Annabel wondered how much more she could take.

CHAPTER ELEVEN

THEY reached the house to find that Marilyn had not returned. Deno said she had been in to lunch and had left soon after a phone call saying she would not be in to dinner.

Colonel Tomes and his wife came and stayed to dinner. They had been to see John after a friend at the club had rung them up to tell them about his collapse. The evening passed pleasantly. When the guests had gone, Annabel and her aunt had just gone into the lounge for a chat before retiring when there was the sound of door chimes, then they heard Deno's voice mingling with a man's deeper tones.

The next moment Deno knocked and entered the room. Annabel stared beyond him through the open door to see Pierre stride into the hall carrying Marilyn in his arms. Her arms were around his neck and her face was hidden in the hollow of his shoulder. Numbly, she watched him go towards the stairs.

Deno said, 'Miss Firbank very upset. Kim-san dead.'

'Dead?' Annabel and her aunt echoed together in a shocked whisper.

Aunt Bea was the first to recover. 'Oh dear!' she exclaimed. 'What happened?'

Deno shook his head. 'Very sudden.'

'It must have been. You'd better ring for the doctor, Deno. Marilyn will be needing a sedative, by the looks of her.' Instantly Bea took charge. 'And Deno, when you've phoned, make tea, please. It's good for shock. I'd better go upstairs to see what I can do.' She turned to her niece, whose heart had taken a precipitate plunge at Deno's words. Dimly Annabel felt her aunt's hand on her arm. 'What about you, dear?' she was saying. 'No use two of us staying up, and you look tired, my pet. Go to bed.'

Annabel hesitated. 'Sure I can't help?'

Bea shook her head. 'A sedative will put Marilyn out for the night.' She sighed. 'What a rotten business! Goodnight, my dear.'

Bea kissed her cheek before running up the stairs to Marilyn's room. Annabel mounted more slowly and, on entering her room, began mechanically to prepare for bed. She was in her pyjamas when the doctor arrived. He did not stay long. When he left Annabel was still standing beside her bed.

She turned the bedclothes down, trying to take it in that Kim was dead. Very sudden, Deno had said. Had he died from drugs or killed himself because Marilyn had walked out on him and was going to marry Pierre? She covered her face with her hands. Oh no! Not suicide, please. It would be an impossible burden for Marilyn to carry about with her all her life if she was responsible for his death.

Annabel knew then that she had to know the truth if she expected to get any sleep. Pierre's deep voice mingling with her aunt's as they went downstairs roused her. Slipping on her dressing gown, she ran a comb through her hair and followed them down.

They were in the lounge, the sound of teacups came through the open door. Annabel paused in the doorway. Her aunt was on the sofa presiding over a low table containing a tray of freshly brewed tea. They looked towards her.

'How is Marilyn?' she asked.

'Sleeping,' said Pierre laconically, drawing out his cigarette case. 'The doctor gave her a sedative.' Without seeming to have moved, he was at her side. 'Come, sit down, *ma chère*.'

'Yes, have a cuppa, dear,' her aunt said. 'I think we all need one.'

Annabel sat down beside her, refusing Pierre's offer of a cigarette. She accepted the tea for something to do with her hands. Pierre, after lighting her aunt's cigarette and his own, lowered himself in a chair opposite to them.

As she looked into her cup, Annabel's voice was little more than a whisper.

'What happened to Kim?' She moistened dry lips. 'I mean ... how did he die?'

Pierre sat back in his chair and exhaled cigarette smoke ceilingwards.

'He died from drugs. Not an overdose—he has been ill for some time. They found him dead in bed at the hotel. He died in his sleep.'

Annabel's next words rushed out on a wave of relief. 'Then he didn't ...' She stopped short, wishing she could recall them, and knowing that her aunt was looking at her curiously.

'Go on,' demanded Pierre. 'You were saying?'

'I ... I thought Kim might have killed himself at a time when he was feeling depressed,' she said, withholding the real reason—that of Marilyn's engagement to himself.

Pierre leaned forward in his chair. 'But so much has happened. Why should you think that, *ma chère*? Kim was the life and soul of the engagement party.'

Annabel almost cringed in her corner of the sofa.

Please, Pierre, her heart begged, don't talk about your engagement party. I can't bear to hear about it. All she wanted was to go to bed and sink into sleep, a sleep of merciful forgetfulness.

It was Aunt Bea who, noticing her pale strained look, said kindly,

'You look all in, my pet. It's sweet of you to be so concerned, but do go back to bed.'

Annabel put down her cup. 'I think I will. It's been quite a day.' She moved towards the door with a smile for them both and bade them good night.

She awoke the following morning feeling unrefreshed after a night of continuous rain. As memory pushed through the waves of sleep she left her bed to wash and dress lethargically. Deno was laying the table on the veranda and her aunt was already there. After the usual polite greetings, Aunt Bea said with some satisfaction,

'Thank goodness Marilyn's parents arrive today. Soon you and I will be settling down to enjoy ourselves.'

Annabel sat back in her chair. The sun shed a liquid heat on her limbs and the garden was beautifully green and fresh after the rain. She stared out at it and unfolded her table napkin with the conviction that she would never enjoy herself again.

'When do the Firbanks arrive?' she asked, reluctant to begin to eat a breakfast for which she had no appetite.

'Around midday. Pierre is meeting them off the plane and bringing them here to lunch.'

Annabel conveyed food to her mouth in a strange half-awake condition. Until that moment she was not thinking at all clearly, but the fact that Pierre would be staying to lunch alerted her as nothing else would have done. One thing was certain—she would not be there. She would have to work out a feasible excuse.

'Do you think Marilyn will be all right? Have you seen her this morning, Aunt Bea?' she asked after taking a drink of coffee to ease the food down her throat.

She asked the questions knowing the first one covered more territory than her aunt was aware of. The possibility of Marilyn taking drugs would never occur to her. If only she knew for certain, she thought unhappily. Someone had to find out before the girl went beyond saving it it was true.

Then painfully it dawned on her that Marilyn was now Pierre's responsibility and that he would soon set about keeping her free from drugs if it happened to be so. Maybe she was looking as sad as she felt, for her aunt's eyes, usually so gentle, hardened on meeting her gaze.

'I neither know nor care. Marilyn is a menace. She's caused her parents distress, messed up your visit and disrupted the household. I can't wait to see the back of her. She was asleep when I looked into her room earlier on.'

After breakfast, when Aunt Bea went to consult Deno about the extra guests for lunch, Annabel went upstairs to see Marilyn. She lay in her bed staring motionless up at the ceiling, her face ashen. The only colour lay in her swollen eyes and her golden hair strewn upon her pillow.

Annabel approached the bed, shocked at the change in her. 'Good morning, Marilyn,' she said. 'I'm sorry to hear about Kim. Is there anything I can do?' Her eyes alighted upon the crumpled handkerchief in the clenched hand on the coverlet. 'A clean handkerchief, perhaps?'

An almost imperceptible shake of the head was the

only answer.

Annabel tried again. 'Aren't you going to drink your coffee? It will ease that aching void inside you.' She picked up the coffee Deno had left on the bedside table. But Marilyn shook her head.

Annabel put down the coffee and after a long silence eventually asked,

'Do you want me to go?'

This time Marilyn gave no sign that she had heard. Awkwardly, Annabel patted the hand gripping the handkerchief.

'I'm sorry to be so inadequate, but Marilyn, please don't be like this when your parents arrive. You'll only distress them greatly, to no purpose. We can't bring Kim back for you. Besides, there's ... there are others to consider who love you dearly.'

Try as she would, Annabel could not bring herself to mention Pierre's name. And while she felt a great compassion for Marilyn in her grief she was also very surprised at her taking Kim's death so much to heart. She had admitted to feeling sorry for him and she was engaged to Pierre. Then why? She was neither plain, lonely or unloved. She still had everything, beauty, health, wealth, doting parents and ... last but not least ... the love of Pierre.

Ironically, Annabel knew she herself would be the happiest girl in the world if she had to walk barefoot as long as she had Pierre. But it was not to be. Bending down, she kissed Marilyn gently on the forehead and left the room, closing the door softly behind her.

She met her aunt coming from the kitchen quarters. She was waving a man's wallet.

'Colonel Tomes,' she explained. 'Deno found it this morning down the side of the chair the Colonel sat in last evening in the lounge. It must have fallen from his pocket. I'll have to ring him. How is Marilyn?'

'Taking it very hard. She's uncommunicative and wants to be left alone,' Annabel said unhappily.

Her aunt looked concerned. 'I'll be relieved when her parents arrive. I'll go up immediately and sit with her. They should be here soon. Has she had any breakfast?'

Annabel shook her head. 'Not even touched her coffee. It might be a good idea to take up a fresh brew for two. She might have some with you.'

The older woman nodded. 'Good idea. But first I must phone the Colonel in case he's missed his wallet and is worried.' She paused as though something had just occurred to her. 'Did I tell you that Pierre is going to invite the Firbanks to his parents' chateau in the Loire valley?'

Annabel shrank inwardly at the quivering pain. She just had to get away then. Desperately, her eyes alighted upon the wallet in her aunt's hand and she was blessing her again for offering a second lifeline.

'No, you didn't tell me,' she said, astonished at her utter calm. 'About the Colonel's wallet, Aunt Bea—I would just love to return it to him. It's an ideal day for a car run and I shall enjoy it. May I?'

Bea consulted her wrist watch and looked rather surprised at the request. 'But, Annabel, you won't be back in time for lunch with the Firbanks and Pierre,' she exclaimed.

'I don't mind if you don't. There'll be four of you for lunch, unless Marilyn decides to join you, which I very much doubt.' Annabel hugged her aunt. 'Please, Aunt Bea. I can take a picnic tea and explore all those delicious little bays on the way back.'

The older woman hesitated, then smiled indulgently. 'All right, if that's what you want. I'll phone the

Colonel to tell him you're coming. Take the big car—you'll enjoy the ride better over the potholes. And while you're going to the kitchen to see about a picnic tea, you might ask Deno to make fresh coffee for two. I must go up to Marilyn.' She handed over the wallet. 'Take care on the roads,' she called as Annabel sped away.

It was a clear, beautiful morning and, as Annabel had said, ideal for motoring. The water in the bay below was at low tide and women were standing in the shallows gathering seaweed, some of which was washed into traps set for the purpose. Annabel drove slowly, enjoying the Japanese scene, the tiny islands in the bay, some mere heaps of rocks, others large enough to house tiny villages with pine trees silhouetted darkly against the blue of the sky.

Beauty was everywhere, from the shimmering bay to the sweeping curve of the headland and along the wooded hilly, inland route. All too soon she was entering the drive of the Colonel's residence and seeing again the lovely garden with the lotus pond, the curving paths of stepping stones across green velvet lawns, the azaleas and the rich lush ground behind the house rising to the hills.

The Colonel received his wallet, beaming with pleasure. 'So good of you to return it personally, my dear,' he said. 'I honestly thought I'd lost it for good. There are one or two little things in it that I carry about with me because they're of sentimental value and I would have hated to have lost them.'

Annabel stayed to lunch, but left soon afterwards to explore the territory on her way back. That afternoon spent meandering through woods where she picked wild flowers and picnicked on a rise commanding a breathtaking view of sea and countryside was a break she had badly needed.

Gradually she came to terms with herself. She felt no bitterness because her own happiness and the dreams she had nurtured were now no more. She knew only a deep sadness of the kind experienced by some-one who, having lost a limb, suddenly resigns herself to living without it. By the time she returned home in the early evening, she had a more virile, unconquer-able look.

There were no cars on the drive when she cruised along it to garage the big car next to her aunt's smaller one. There was no sign of life either as the house lay dreaming in the sun. With her arms filled with the wild flowers, Annabel stopped in the front porch to shed her footwear and wriggle her toes into the house shoes on the step. Silence greeted her as she crossed the hall to peep into the lounge. But the figure rising from a chair when she paused on the threshold was much bigger than Aunt Bea.

Her heart leapt suffocatingly in her throat and con-tinued to beat in thick heavy strokes, as their eyes met across the room.

'So the wood nymph returns. Do come in, *chérie*.' Pierre sauntered towards her across the room, his mocking gaze narrowing at her obvious reluctance as she stood there with her arms filled with fragrant flowers just inside the room. Her face was deathly pale and he frowned at the dismay and fear as she uttered no word.

He had almost reached her when she found her tongue. 'Shouldn't you be with the Firbanks? Where is Aunt Bea, and why isn't your car on the drive?'

The words tumbled from her pale lips in one dis-mayed breath. A gleam came in his eyes and his mouth quirked at the corners.

179

'*Tiens*, which question must I answer first? Shall we remove the flowers in order to see you? All I can see at the moment are two very blue frightened eyes.'

When his hands reached out Annabel gathered herself together like a cornered animal making a desperate bid for freedom.

'I'll take them to Deno.'

Annabel turned with the words, but quick as she was, Pierre was quicker. Moving with lightning rapidity, he closed the door and blocked her way.

'And now, *ma belle*, the flowers, *s'il te plaît*.'

She started a little at the curt peremptoriness of his voice and relinquished the flowers, which he laid down on a nearby table. The next moment his hand had closed on her arm with a close, vital grip.

'Come, sit down, and do not look so afraid,' he commanded.

But still Annabel hung back. 'It's Aunt Bea, isn't it? Something has happened to her or John? Please tell me, Pierre. Don't keep me in suspense!'

Annabel had not lifted her head, but she felt his anger as she kept her eyes glued to the hand on her arm. His grip tightened. His voice was curt.

'So you say Pierre. For a moment I half expected you to say Monsieur. I refuse to say anything more until you sit down and we talk like two rational beings.'

After a slight hesitation, Annabel allowed him to pilot her to a chair near the glass sliding doors overlooking the garden. They had been closed and he leaned back against the framework to look down at her.

He began, 'We will first dispense with your aunt. She has gone to spend the afternoon with John in my car because her own refused to start. Marilyn has gone with her parents to their villa.'

He had spoken with the air of a man being tolerant against his will. Now he was frowning almost savagely. His hands were thrust into his pockets.

'And now you will please tell me why I should not call upon you as a friend? What is so unusual about it that you immediately assume something has happened and that I am the bearer of bad news?'

Annabel was breathing nervously and she subdued her agitation with an effort. She met his eyes steadily.

'You don't think it's unusual for an engaged man to leave his fiancée at the time when she most needs him in order to visit another woman?' she asked quietly.

He was astonished. 'Engaged?' he echoed, his face growing stern. 'What absurdity is this?'

Annabel's nerves were stretched and quivering, but her clear eyes did not waver from his. 'It's no absurdity, and well you know it! You're taking the Firbanks home to meet your family.'

He said with a directness oddly disconcerting, 'The Firbanks are leaving almost immediately for the States where a certain young man who was once very close to Marilyn is waiting to comfort her.'

Her blue eyes widened up at him. 'And you don't mind?'

'Mind?' He savoured the words as though it was distasteful. 'Mind?' he repeated. 'Why should I mind? If you mean about Marilyn, she was never anything more to me than a friend.'

Annabel was very white. 'But she wore your ring, and I saw you together in the bar of the hotel drinking champagne.'

'She did not wear my ring. It was Kim's ring. He had moved into the hotel that evening and was up in his room supervising the arrival of his gear. He came down later. Marilyn became engaged to him because the doctor had told her he had not long to live. You know he was taking drugs? He died in his sleep. One of the hotel staff found him when he failed to appear at lunch time.'

'Oh dear! Poor Marilyn. No wonder she'd taken it so hard. I thought she was engaged to you. I'm sure Aunt Bea did too.' The last words were flung at him defiantly. 'You were always with her—and I did see you kiss her goodnight.'

He smiled. 'There was never anything to it. We were both free to enjoy each other's company. Marilyn was a trifle mixed up and I helped to sort her out.'

Annabel's arms were straight down beside her, her fingers curled around the edges of the seat. It was all so heartbreakingly clear. She had forgotten that Pierre was not the marrying kind. Marilyn had been just another affair, as she herself had been, in between assignments. Scarcely aware of what she was doing, she left the chair and walked slowly to where he had placed the wild flowers on a table. She touched the delicate petal of a small blue flower, knowing it would wither like her heart seemed to have done.

'So you came to say goodbye,' she said tonelessly. 'You said you had another assignment. I can think of no other reason why you should be here when you could easily have driven Aunt Bea to John's club, which also is your own.'

'Can you not, *mignonne*?' he said just behind her. 'Are you not curious why I said it is the most important assignment of my life?'

With every nerve trembling at his nearness, Annabel stiffened her defences. 'Your assignments will always be the most important thing in your life. Why should this one be any different?'

'Because you will be in it.'

She swung round to face him then, eyes blazing. Bitterly, she said,

'Am I to be your next affair now that Marilyn has gone? I suppose Aunt Bea has told you I'm not in love with Francis Kerrison and you still regard me as fair game.' Her voice trembled.

Pierre saw her rising agitation and subdued it with a gentle smile.

'Why do you think I came to Japan?' he asked softly.

She met his look with a brave face. 'Not to meet me.'

'Why else? After we parted two years ago I was never the same. You had taken part of me with you. You kept coming between my first love, my job, and were in all my waking hours. I was away from Paris for the best part of two years, not wanting to go back and find you gone. I kept telling myself that I would forget you, that you could be married and starting a family. But it was no use. I returned to Paris two months ago and asked your parents for your address. They told me you were going to spend a holiday in Japan—so I came.'

Annabel gazed at him with wide eyes. Her lips felt stiff and cold.

'To play about with Marilyn,' she said stonily.

'No, to bide my time, after you told me you had grown up and was not interested in me any longer. *Mignonne*,' he breathed, his hands at her waist, 'I never wanted you more than in that moment.'

Annabel tilted her chin. 'Well, so I've grown up.'

His look dwelt upon her, caressed her, drew her

with a great tenderness.

'*Mignonne*, as one grown-up to another, will you marry me?'

Annabel stood quite still. Her astonished expression changed to one of wonder and delight. Then, with a sudden moan, she pushed him away.

'No, oh no!' she cried. 'We can't ever marry, Pierre. I could marry you, but you would give me nothing of yourself that mattered. Your work would always come first. I want what you can't give. You've no right to ask me on those terms.'

Pierre's eyes flashed. '*Mon Dieu*! Is that how you think I love you?'

He pulled her to him savagely and kissed her fiercely on the lips in arrogant, searching, tender kisses, kisses of the kind a man gives to the one woman he has taken for his own, whom he has every right to kiss and wants to go on kissing for the rest of his life. The furnace of his passion seemed to fuse them together for a very long time. She felt the beat of his heart thudding into her as his lips moved down to her neck.

'*Chérie*,' he murmured, 'I have resigned from my job and I am taking up writing. I have had one book published about my adventures and it has been enormously successful. Say you love me.'

He lifted his head to see her blue eyes swimming with tears, her lips trembling. 'Are you sure, Pierre?' she asked piteously. 'No regrets because I've never stopped loving you from the night we met?'

His dark eyes laughed down into hers with passionate intensity.

'*Mignonne*,' he declared softly, 'do you know what I have discovered? I have discovered that changing course mid-stream gives one an entirely new lease of life. And with the beloved partner it promises a joy so great that I shall cherish it for the rest of my life.'

He had to kiss her again then, crushing her against him in all her slender sweetness as he savoured the salt of her tears and all the loving beneath.

He said, his voice not quite steady, 'You look radiant, *mignonne*.' His eyes glowed like live coals burning down into hers. He looked incredibly boyish, exceedingly happy and so strong and virile.

Annabel, her face rosy from his kisses, framed his face in her hands and pushed back a truant lock of the crisp dark hair from his forehead.

'So do you, dear Pierre. Tell me, why did you invite the Firbanks to your home? What if they had accepted?'

'Jealous?' he teased. 'I thought it would be good for them all to get away for a while before returning to the States. I did not expect them to stay to our wedding, so I suggested them going to stay at my parents' place for a while. It is beautiful there, *mignonne*. You will love it.' He laughed. 'They were a little taken aback when I told them that not only was I hoping to marry you but I had already got the ring and the man to perform the ceremony. He is a bishop staying at my club and he has consented to marry us.'

Annabel gasped. 'Pierre!' she exclaimed. 'Whatever did they say?'

'It certainly shook Marilyn out of her lethargic state. It was she who suggested lending us the villa for our honeymoon. I accepted. They are leaving early tomorrow for the States.' He grinned. 'Did I tell you we are being married tomorrow afternoon at a little church not far from here? Everything has been arranged.'

'But, Pierre, it's so ... so sudden!' she gasped.

'After two years? You must be joking,' he said against her lips.

THE OMNIBUS
Has Arrived!

A GREAT NEW IDEA
From HARLEQUIN

OMNIBUS — The 3-in-1 HARLEQUIN
only $1.75 per volume

Here is a great new exciting idea from Harlequin. THREE GREAT ROMANCES — complete and unabridged — BY THE SAME AUTHOR — in one deluxe paperback volume — for the unbelievably low price of only $1.75 per volume.

We have chosen some of the finest works of four world-famous authors . . .

CATHERINE AIRLIE

VIOLET WINSPEAR ②

KATHRYN BLAIR

ROSALIND BRETT

. . . and reprinted them in the 3-in-1 Omnibus. Almost 600 pages of pure entertainment for just $1.75 each. A TRULY "JUMBO" READ!

These four Harlequin Omnibus volumes are now available. The following pages list the exciting novels by each author.

Climb aboard the Harlequin Omnibus now! The coupon below is provided for your convenience in ordering.

Catherine Airlie

Omnibus

This author's fine books have become famous throughout North America, and are greatly anticipated by readers of romance all over the world. The three stories chosen for this volume highlight her unusual talent of combining the elements of compassion and suspense in one exceptional novel.

. . . . CONTAINING:

DOCTOR OVERBOARD . . . on board a luxury liner, cruising between the Canary Islands, Trinidad and Barbados, a young Scot, Mairi Finlay, is facing a traumatic experience, torn between her growing affection for the young ship's surgeon, and her duty to her employer who has set her an impossible task . . . (#979).

NOBODY'S CHILD . . . from London England, we are taken to a medieval castle, the Schloss Lamberg, situated on the outskirts of the City of Vienna, to brush shoulders with the aristocracy of the music world. Amidst all of this beauty, a young girl, Christine Dainton, is submerged in the romance of a lifetime with one of the most admired men in the world . . . (#1258).

A WIND SIGHING . . . Jean Lorimer's life has always been happy here, on the small Hebridean Island of Kinnail, owned by the Lorimer family for centuries. Now, Jean and her mother are grief stricken on the death of her father. They will surely lose their home too, for Kinnail was always inherited by the eldest male in the family, whose arrival they expect any day now (#1328).

$1.75 per volume

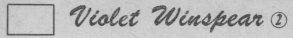

Violet Winspear ②

Omnibus

Only once in a very long time, does an author such as Violet Winspear emerge from the hosts of writers of popular novels. Her effortless portrayal of the human emotions experienced in romantic conflict has contributed greatly to her acknowledgement as one of the finest writers of romance in the world.

. . . . CONTAINING:

BRIDE'S DILEMMA . . . on the beautiful island of Ste. Monique, young Tina Manson fought hard to preserve her newfound happiness in a blissful marriage to the man she had loved since their very first meeting. But there was someone else who loved him, and whose endless scheming proved powerful enough to crush Tina's world . . . (#1008).

TENDER IS THE TYRANT . . . Lauri Garner, almost eighteen years old, had such an alarming innocence about her. She had been dancing with the great di Corte Ballet Company only a short time when she fell in love with Signor di Corte. Unknown to Lauri, he sought only to mould her into another Prima Donna Travilla—no matter what the cost . . . (#1208).

THE DANGEROUS DELIGHT . . . it would take a few hours before the coach could proceed. Faye was grateful for the break in her journey from Lisbon, and the chance of a short walk. To be discovered as a trespasser on the grounds of the estate of none other than the Conde Vincente de Rebelo Falcao was an innocent crime—the consequences of which were most serious . . . (#1344).

$1.75 per volume

Kathryn Blair

Omnibus

Kathryn Blair's outstanding work has become famous and most appreciated by those who seek real-life characters against backgrounds which create and hold the interest throughout the entire story, thus producing the most captivating and memorable romantic novels available today.

. . . . CONTAINING:

DOCTOR WESTLAND . . . Tess Carlen is invited to recuperate in Tangier after suffering almost fatal injuries in an accident. On the voyage, Tess agrees to look after a small boy, and to deliver him to his father on arrival. By doing so, Tess becomes deeply embroiled in the mystery of Tangier which cloaks Dr. Philip Westland and his young son . . . (#954).

BATTLE OF LOVE . . . on the death of her husband, Catherine and her small son are offered a home by her father-in-law, Leon Verender, co-guardian of the boy. Chaos develops rapidly between them, caused by conflicting ideas on how to raise a child. Leon's scheming fiancée then delivers an ultimatum to Catherine—making life for her and her son impossible . . . (#1038).

FLOWERING WILDERNESS . . . a rubber plantation in Africa was no place for a woman as far as David Raynor was concerned. Nicky Graham had a great deal of courage, and she was determined to stay. Alas, before long, Nicky was forced to leave, but now she was very much in love with the same David Raynor . . . (#1148).

$1.75 per volume

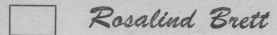

Rosalind Brett

Omnibus

A writer with an excitingly different appeal that transports the reader on a journey of enchantment to far-off places where warm, human people live in true to life circumstances, Miss Brett's refreshing touch to the age-old story of love, continues to fascinate her ever-increasing number of faithful readers.

. . . . CONTAINING:

THE GIRL AT WHITE DRIFT . . . Jerry Lake had travelled from England to Canada to live with her unknown guardian, Dave Farren. On arrival, Mr. Farren drove Jerry to his home, White Drift Farm, explaining that a few months' farm life would strengthen and build a fine body. To her utter horror, Jerry realized that this man thought she was a boy! . . . (#1101).

WINDS OF ENCHANTMENT . . . in Kanos, Africa, in surroundings of intense heat, oppressive jungle, insects and fever, Pat Brading faces the heartbreak of losing her father. The acute depression and shock she suffers in the following months gradually subside, and slowly she becomes aware that she is now married to a man who revolts her and whom she must somehow, escape . . . (#1176).

BRITTLE BONDAGE . . . when Venetia wrote the letter which had brought Blake Garrard immediately to her side in a time of need, she had felt great sorrow and bewilderment. Now, some time and a great deal of pain later, it was the contents of another letter which must drive her away from him. Only now, Blake was her husband . . . (#1319).

$1.75 per volume